Again the short hairs crawled at the back of Parry's neck as he strained his ears, trying to isolate any alien sound out of the wind, the neighing, the barking.

Nothing. And nothing for them to do but fall back, retreat from the unseen menace that clearly had them at its mercy. God . . . what was it? A deadly game?

Again the crash of a rifle.

One of the parlor's front windows buckled in a shower of glass. Parry let go with his pistol at a stab of gunflame out by the coop. It was like firing at a ghost.

They were in total darkness, and the bucko lad out there would show himself by starlight if he moved out of the shadow.

But he didn't. . . .

A Killer is Waiting

T.V. Olsen

FAWCETT GOLD MEDAL • NEW YORK

CHAPTER ONE

WILL PARRY WAS TIRED AND HE WAS A HEAVY SLEEPER. Barney's loud barking pulled him out of the well of sleep by grudging degrees. With an irritable grunt, he pushed back the blankets, sat up in bed, and swung his legs to the floor.

Starshine from the window touched various objects in the room with dim sheens and shadows. The shock of icy floorboards under Parry's bare feet cleared the shreds of sleep from his brain as he moved to the window and squinted out at the ranchyard under the dull starlight. He couldn't make out a damned thing this side of the house, but Barney was keeping up that ferocious din and he'd better investigate. Parry groped for the chair where he'd draped his clothes, barked his shins on the seat and swore sleepily. He laboriously climbed into his pants, then sat down on the bed to tug on his boots, stamping his sockless feet into the cold leather.

Leah's warm, mounded shape stirred beside him. She said drowsily, "What is it?"

"Lord knows. Something. He's racketing his fool head off."

"Want me to light the lamp?"

"No. Stay set. I'll rouse Linc and we'll have a look."

Parry stood up, awkwardly ramming the tails of his nightshirt into his pants with one hand. In fifteen years of making do with one hand and a hook he'd learned to do

1

most things in about half the time a man with two good hands could do them. But he couldn't easily handle a lamp and a gun at the same time.

He pulled open the top drawer of the commode, took out his Colt's Civilian Model Single Action .45, then fumbled his way over to the door. As he opened it, a bull's-eye lantern made bobbing beams along the corridor walls. His son Linc already stood at the open door of his room, lantern held in one hand, his Winchester rifle in the other hand pointed at the floor. He, too, had on pants and boots.

"Old Barn is sure bugling to raise the dead, Pa. I better go with you."

Tim, the nine-year-old, pushed out past the tall, gangling form of his brother. He scrubbed at one eye with his fist. "Me, too."

"You stay set, buckshot," Will Parry told him. "Back to bed with you. Linc, you go down ahead. Hold that lantern higher, will you?"

As the two of them headed for the stairway, Tim muttering after them "Aw shise" (a euphemism that Parry let him get by with even if Leah didn't), the door to Ariel's room opened. She stood in her nightdress, curling her toes against the cold floor. The mass of her red-gold hair tumbled over one shoulder as she tipped her head, blinking sleepily.

"What is it, Daddy?"

Parry said, "Tell you that after we find out, sis," and went down the stairs behind Linc. The swaying lantern made banked, guttering shadows to the sides and front of them as they crossed the dark front parlor, lifted the night bar off the front door, and went out.

Barney was straining at the light chain that anchored him to a porch column, rearing and lunging back and forth, still yapping crazily. Parry said mildly, "Settle down, Barn." The big hound promptly quieted. He stood looking at them, his stiff tail wagging, but his arousal was still evident in the bristling ridge of hair along his forward spine.

"Hold still a minute, Pa."

Parry halted beside his son, both of them listening intently. At nineteen, Linc had outdoorsman's senses sharper than his father's had ever been. Studying out a situation of any kind, Linc would comb every detail of the scene for what it might hold. His head was back like a hunting dog's, his profile keen against the star-frosted sky.

A chill spring wind coasting down off the high Never-summer Range bit through Will Parry's nightshirt. He shivered, flexing his hand around the rubber grips of his Colt, while he sent a circling glance across the dark blocks of the outbuildings, solid and silent against the clear night.

Linc shook his head. "Can't pick out a blamed thing."

"Maybe that damn fox after the chickens again."

"No sound from the coop, Pa."

"We best have a look anyway."

Barney sent a plaintive whine after them as they tramped across the yard. Now lamplight showed in the windows of the bunkhouse nearly fifty yards away and the door scraped open, carving a long saffron rectangle out of the yard shadows. Truitt Barrows came out first, lean and big-shouldered against the light, and he was toting the lamp. After him, then moving up to flank him, came grizzled and wiry Bill Soholt and the crabbed, drag-footed form of Genardo Menocal, who was muttering angrily in his cracked, surly old voice, most of it a run of Spanish epithets.

Truitt said, "Hey, boss," and he and the other two hands came up to join Parry and Linc, who had pulled up to wait for them. All three were half-dressed. A six-gun dangled in Truitt's left fist.

"Did you hear anything?" Parry asked.

"Just your houn' dog noising 'er up." Truitt's bland wide

face wore a sleepy scowl. "What'n hell is it? Never heard 'im go off just that way that I can remember."

A sharp gust of wind, then a banging sound, made all five men jerk half around to face the chicken house a hundred feet away. All Parry could see was the dim box of its outline, but the door was swinging loose and open.

"You reckon," said Bill Soholt in his poker-faced way, "that a fox reached up and unlatched that coop door?"

"Oh, hell, something a sight bigger," Truitt said. "Bear? Maybe a hungry Injun?"

"Or," Parry said dryly, "the latch slipped and the wind did the rest. Come on."

The five of them approached the coop warily, the old Mexican quietly and steadily grumbling. Parry knew Barney wasn't likely to go off like a firecracker over just a banging door. A sense of something baleful and unseen, something he couldn't lay a name to, prickled the short hairs at the back of his neck. *What?* He gave himself an irritated answer: nerves, the cold and windy darkness, the suddenness of being dragged from sleep.

All the same he felt a need for excessive caution.

Parry was in the lead as they pulled up short of the coop door. The crossbeams of lamp and lantern, held well to the right and left of the doorway, swiftly illumined the whole interior of the coop.

"Goddlemighty and Satan's socks," said Truitt Barrows.

The inside of the chicken house looked as if a tornado had hit it. The bodies of a dozen birds lay scattered about, dead or dying, in grotesquely twisted positions. A few still made feeble croakings and wing-flutters, but their eyes were glazing into death. The dirt floor was scattered with feathers, but not a trace of blood showed.

Bill Soholt was the first to move. He stepped into the shed and picked up a motionless bird, turning it in his callused hands. "This 'un's neck's been wrung. Twisted around clean as a whistle. Same with the others, I reckon."

"Bring 'em out," Parry said. "Lay 'em in a row. Linc, keep watch."

All the birds had been treated in a like way. Five of them still flapped and croaked weakly. Truitt said, "Why, this here's a crazy thing. Jesus. Take a crazy man to do it."

"The live ones is done for," said Bill Soholt. "Want me to finish 'em? Reach in the throat, you can cut a vein. I done it that way sometimes."

Will Parry nodded absently, his thoughts already twisting another way. "Yes. Do that."

Soholt took out a clasp knife and opened the small blade. As he bent to the task, he said mildly, "You run afoul of any loonies lately, Will? I sure ain't that I know of."

Parry shook his head.

The grisly shock of the tableau gripped him less with a question of who than of why. Someone had got inside the shed and closed the door and done the job with a swift, deadly efficiency. A quick seizing, a sudden twist by two powerful hands. The terrified gabbling of the birds had roused Barney, but the work was done in a flash . . . twelve times over. In utter darkness. By a single man? With an almost unbelievable swiftness? Parry didn't have to think about the answer to any of these. It was flat and intuitive and chilling: *Yes*.

"Two birds missing," observed Soholt as he straightened up now, wiping the blade and his bloody hands on a ragged bandanna. "There was fourteen."

"Jesus A'mighty," Truitt said. "Leastways it wasn't no h'ant that done it."

"Never said it was." The flesh at the corners of Soholt's blue eyes crinkled with bleak amusement. "How does your figuring run, boy?"

"Well," Truitt said seriously, "carried off a couple birds,

didn't he? Makes sense he stole 'em to eat, don't it? No ha'nt has to eat. Had to be a live man."

"You don't say."

"Maybe," husked old Genardo, "it was a *nagual*."

Truitt grunted. "*Nah*—what's 'at? That one of your spick something or others?"

"Is no ghost," Genardo said. "Is a man who turns to an animal. He change as he want to. Change back as he want to. The *nagual*. In old Mexico the people don' laugh at such things."

"Aw Jesus." Truitt chuckled with nervous disgust. "All that silly-shit Mex stuff. Ain't no white man with sense holds to that. Now a ha'nt, that's different."

"You don't say," said Bill Soholt.

"Betcher ass. My old pap, he seen the ghost of his pap once, swore it on the Book. Pap used to ship on a mean load of redeye betimes, but not that time, he was sober as—"

Parry said irritably, "Truitt, put a cinch on your jaw." He was watching Linc down on one knee a few yards away, lantern held low as he inspected the ground.

"You find anything, son?"

"Nary sign of a ha'nt," Linc said gravely. "Man track here. A real live one, like Truitt says. Come have a look, but don't tromp around more than you need to. Could be more sign about."

The men gathered around the pool of light. They saw a lone moccasin print deeply indented in a patch of moist scuffed earth.

Truitt whispered, "God, he's a whopper, ain't he? Big ole son. Leastways he got damn big feet."

"Cheyenne moccasin made that track," Soholt said. "No other cut like it."

"Still." Genardo bobbed his head, his old eyes glinting like black beads. "Could be a *nagual*."

"Boy." Truitt was still nervously mirthful. "Who's gonna believe a bunch a dumb shit like that."

Parry felt an increasing irritation. Ghosts. Haunts. Werebeasts. Yet he felt the same nameless awareness of something eerie, unexplainable. Truitt had said it the first time. This sudden, wanton act added up to pure craziness.

"Well, he's a big son sure enough," Bill Soholt said matter-of-factly. "Tall big or wide big. But heavy. Lot of weight come down on that track."

Parry straightened up, turning away from the dry smell of old chicken shit, the wet stench of fresh blood. "We better search the other buildings," he said. "Bill, Genardo, get yourself some guns and a couple more lanterns. We—"

Linc put a hand on his arm. "Wait, Pa. Hark."

Parry listened intently. The wind was gusting up around them, whistling through the leafless branches of isolated trees. Then he caught the sharp, restive sounds of horses in the main corral adjoining the stable. But from where they were the shape of the corral was lost against the black spires of a fir grove off behind it.

Barney began to bay frantically again.

"He's back of the corral," Bill Soholt said. "Or," he added as the corralled animals began to mill nervously, whickering and blubbering, "maybe he's got in there with 'em, by God!"

"We'll move up each side of the corral," murmured Parry. "Bill, you take Truitt and Genardo around by the left and go back of the stable. Keep together. No telling what we're up against. Linc and I'll take the right. See if we can force him into the open. Lantern, Linc."

Still watching the corral and grove, Parry thrust out his right arm, the one that ended in a stump. Linc hesitated and Parry said impatiently, "You'll need both hands for the rifle."

"You reckon there'll be a need, Pa?"

"If I say the word, yes. Come on."

Linc hung the lantern's bale over his father's forearm. They separated now, the three crewmen skirting off to the left with Truitt's lamp bobbing out their way. As he and Linc circled to the right, Parry thought that he should have given Soholt his pistol. That way, with his one hand free, he could have steadied the lantern better. It was always his instinct, Parry knew wryly, to take command, to take on a shade more than he was able to. Something else, though: anyone holding a light would make the plainest target and, come to that, he wanted it to be him, not his son.

They were close to the corral poles now, able to make out some of the thrashing confusion inside, and he awkwardly beamed the bull's-eye lantern among the panicked, snorting animals.

Then came the sudden report of a rifle.

The lantern was torn from his arm stump by the bullet's impact. It went bounding away, hit the ground with a tinkling crash of shattered glass and metal, and the flame tattered out in the wind.

Linc brought up his Winchester and fired at the livid spurt of gunflame that marked the shot's source—toward the right back side of the corral. There was no return fire. Any sound from that direction was lost in the noise of wind and barking, the horses' excitement, Truitt bawling a question at the top of his voice.

Both the Parrys froze in place now, Will cuddling the numbed stump of his arm against his chest, holding his pistol pointed at the darkness, with nothing to shoot at.

And the intruder's second shot came. Swift as a shadow, he'd changed position. This time Parry couldn't see the powderflash, but the shot came from the corral's other back side, and Truitt's lamp was wiped out as its glass chimney exploded. Truitt's yells diminished into savage oaths as, maybe fifty yards to the Parrys' right, he opened up wildly with his six-gun.

Truitt's hammer fell on a spent chamber.

"Stay where you are!" Parry roared. "Shut up, Truitt!"

All of them were silent now, motionless but caught in the faint starlight. The intruder remained unseen and—except in the unlikely event that one of Truitt's blind shots had found him—could still pick them off. Shooting accurately enough just to take out the lamps, he could have potted one of them easily.

Again the short hairs crawled at the back of Parry's neck as he strained his ears, trying to isolate any alien sound out of the rush of the wind, the neighing, the barking.

Nothing. And nothing for them to do but fall back, retreat from the unseen menace that clearly had them at its mercy. God . . . what was this? A deadly game?

Parry yelled at the others to break for the house, make for it as fast as they could. The bunkhouse was too far away. And they should stay together.

Catching Linc roughly by the shoulder, he shoved the boy ahead of him, using his own bulk to shield his son as they headed for the house at a bent-over run. Coming after them at an angle, Truitt was close on their heels as they hit the porch. Parry's backward glance showed him that Soholt was some yards behind, supporting the gimpy-legged Genardo as the old Mexican hobbled wildly, sputtering curses.

"Move it, Bill!" Parry roared.

Pausing just long enough to slip Barney's chain, he charged across the porch as Linc got the door open and dived inside, Parry and the dog and Truitt right behind him. Parry held the door wide as Bill Soholt and Genardo came piling through, then slammed it shut and dropped the night bar in place.

From the floor above came the excited voices of the two younger children. And Leah's, telling them to be still and stay put. Then Leah came down the stairs, the skirt of her nightdress caught in one hand, a lamp raised in the other. Its sallow rays wavered through the parlor and Parry moved swiftly to the stairway and took the lamp from her.

"Will—!"

"Get back up there," he told her. "Get the kids down on the floor. All of you stay flat down—"

Again the crash of a rifle.

One of the parlor's front windows buckled in a shower of glass. Parry motioned fiercely and Leah turned wordlessly and ran up the stairs. He went swiftly to the walnut gun cabinet as Linc, crouched by the broken window, sent a shot into the night. Parry set the lamp on the floor and opened the cabinet door to let Truitt and Soholt and Genardo grab rifles from the gunrack while he broke out boxes of ammunition from the shelf above.

"Have to see to all sides—" he told them just as another bullet shattered the other front-facing window. Impatiently he waited as they loaded the weapons, then blew out the lamp. He told Truitt and Soholt to get to the dining room and kitchen and cover those areas.

As he spoke, a shot smashed a second floor window on this side. From upstairs came Ariel's girlish squeal of shock and fear; it wasn't a wail of pain. Linc was firing steadily from his window and Parry heard him mouth a solitary "Damn!"

Parry joined him at the window and let go with his pistol at a stab of gunflame out by the coop. It was like firing at a ghost. The other second floor window at the front of the house collapsed.

For the moment no more shots came, but Parry didn't dare hope that he'd taken the man out. Temporarily, at least, maybe they had an advantage. They were in total darkness and the bucko lad out there would show himself by starlight if he moved out of shadow.

But he didn't.

They waited in the chill, flesh-quilling dark. The horses had quieted. No sound came but the wind and Barney stalking nervously around the room, rumbling deep-chested growls.

Suddenly the parlor's one side window burst in a jangle of glass that merged with gunroar. Genardo, crouched at that window, yelled imprecations and pumped shots into the night. Two more outside shots and Parry heard the upstairs windows on that side go.

For the next fifteen minutes the intruder kept up a vicious, easy pattern of attack. He smashed each first story window on all sides of the house, never missing a shot. He fired once from each position he took, then was gone from it before return shots could search out the blossoms of his gunfire. When he'd finished with the lower window sashes, he made another circle of the house and methodically took out the upper panes.

Continually shifting their own positions, the men inside tried to follow his moves. Often they fired back. But he changed his vantages erratically. Always he clung to wherever shadows were deepest, outbuildings or trees or the woodpile. And when the last pane of glass was shattered, he quit.

Yet they waited tensely on another move.

They waited for unending minutes . . . and the minutes dragged into hours. Was he still out there? Nobody offered to go out and draw the assailant's fire, and Parry would have squelched any such notion.

They waited in the dark, sometimes changing their positions at various windows on the ground floor, but saying little. Glass littered the floors of every room, crunching constantly under their boots. Both Truitt and Genardo did a lot of quiet swearing. Parry went upstairs and made sure nobody was hurt.

Bill Soholt, however, had taken a shard of flying glass in the face. It had laid open his left cheek from chin to temple and the cut had bled badly. Soholt stoically kept at his duty, holding a series of strips from the kitchen ragbag over the cut, each piece of cloth quickly soaking through.

It was a cold watch, drafts of night wind blasting through the broken windows and through the whole house. Leah found enough coats and blankets for everyone, but a man would still be chilled too stiff to handle a gun if he didn't get up and stir about now and then.

Parry joined Soholt at a kitchen window where he was crouched, holding his rifle on the sill with one hand and a bloody cloth to his cheek with the other. Dropping wearily on his haunches beside him, Parry said, "Better get that sewed up pretty soon."

"She'll wait," Soholt said. "Taken a sight of scars in my time that never got stitched."

"You ever run out of blood in your time?"

"Be light out soon. Won't have to watch so close. Can tend to 'er then." Soholt glanced at him. "Back in the war, you ever feel like a sitting duck, Will?"

"Sometimes. Never like this."

"Me neither."

A chill wet touch at the back of his neck made Parry jerk and grunt, "Jesus!"

Barney had padded up unnoticed and cold-nosed him. Parry rubbed the hound's neck, feeling the soundless, ongoing burr of growls in his throat. Looking at Soholt, he made out the other's grin.

"Spooks a body for sure," said the grizzled foreman, and Parry grinned back.

Soholt had been with him since he'd begun to develop his small horse-and-cattle ranch, right after the war. Parry remembered that first night on his newly bought land, after their arrival in Chinook Basin. They were fresh out of

Illinois: he and Leah and six-year-old Linc and Ariel, still a baby in arms, sitting around a wind-gusted campfire when Soholt, a grubline drifter, had ridden in and said a polite howdy and then, following the custom, had waited for an invitation to light down and eat.

Parry had hired him almost on the spot, and Bill Soholt's drifting days were over. Bill was forty-six then and of a mind to toast the last itch out of his toes by a warm hearth, as he'd put it, for the rest of his days. But Soholt wasn't a man for idling; he was a hard worker who'd matched Parry's own ambitious energy in building up his WP outfit. Working cattle or raising horses, Soholt knew both trades from the ground up. Parry, city-raised, had absorbed Bill's range lore like a sponge. It had been invaluable from the start, and there still seemed no end to it.

At sixty-one, Soholt was as wiry and vigorous as ever. The years had frosted his dark hair, but hadn't stiffened his lean frame by a jot that Parry could tell.

"Be light in another hour," Bill said. "Gray light anyhow. Enough to go out and have a look by."

Parry shook his head. "We don't step outside, any of us, till it's full dawn. Then you and Linc can look for tracks."

"Reckon he's well gone by now. Been three hour."

"We don't know it."

Soholt grunted, shifted on his haunches and eased his rifle to the floor. "He was playin' pat-a-cake with us, Will. Any time when we was out there, he could of taken out any of us."

Parry combed his hand through the thick ruff of his beard, nodding tiredly. His right arm rested on his knee, and attached to the stump of that arm now was the leather jacket he'd fitted over it during one of his trips upstairs. He took the jacket off at night for good reason: a pointed steel hook a half-inch thick and eight inches long projected from it. A glimmer of starlight traced its wicked curve in the darkness.

Even hunkered down, Will Parry was an impressive hulk of a man. Standing, he just reached six feet tall, but the sheer breadth of him when he moved gave him the swinging, thickset gait of a bear. Yet it would be hard to pinch an ounce of fat off any part of him. His broad face, framed by the thick curling blackness of his hair and beard, was both tough and pleasant. The deep blue of his eyes was as tranquil as a summer pool, but could ice up like the surface of one in winter. That look, taken with his size, had always been enough to stop cold most anyone who'd ever taken a notion to try conclusions with him.

But nobody had tried any for a good many years. All the troublesome times of his youth had been left back East. There'd been the war, of course. But that was something else.

"There's a mighty big why to all this," Soholt said.

"Or maybe no why at all. Maybe just a damn crazy man's game. Kill the chickens, shoot out a couple lights and a lot of windows, then just quit for the same reason he started. No reason," Parry said.

"Asked you if you run afoul of any loonies of late," Soholt said. "If you don't recollect none, could still be a man with a reason. Mean man with a strong grudge, say. You ever make an Injun mad?"

Parry thought of Little Crow's band, a straggle of peaceable Cheyennes who ranged about Chinook Basin and the Neversummer foothills year-round, making camps where they could hunt, fish, trap, or cultivate gardens as the season dictated. They'd camped often on WP land, and Parry had always maintained good relations with them, making small gifts of trade wares, eating at their fires. Little Crow was his friend.

"Any man can put on a pair of Cheyenne moccasins."

Soholt nodded. "And this don't read like no Injun work.

'Cept for stealing a couple chickens. You hear anything concerning Virg of late?"

Parry had already considered Virg Bollinger as a more than likely candidate. Bollinger had worked as his horse-handler for less than a year. He was a crafty, quiet man, a seasoned trapper of wild horses, and he knew how to take the edges off them as well. But he was a shade too rough in his breaking ways, and a few months back he'd lost his temper with a captured wildling that had given him a nasty spill. Virg had snubbed the animal to a post and worked him over with a doubled piece of strapleather and, when Parry caught him at it, had refused to desist.

Parry had hit him, just once.

"Not a thing," Parry said slowly. "Only talk I picked up was, Virg drifted out of the country after he mended."

"You missed a beat there," Soholt said. "You don't go in a saloon enough, Will. Virg drifted for a spell, but he's back. I was in the Red Star last Saturday and one of the boys told me Virg had been in a couple nights before. Was drinking it up and bad-mouthing you. Said he aimed to settle accounts with you, wait and see."

"You never mentioned it."

"Didn't seem worth the saying. Virg was never a talker 'cept he'd get winded up when he got redeye in him. Just a lot more of his wind, I figured." Soholt chuckled a little, shaking his head. "Man, you laid it to him. You coldcocked the son of a bitch into the middle of next week. Took him damn near that long to come out of it. His jaw's healed now, they say, but he's still shy most of his front teeth. Didn't surprise me too much you could manage it, Will. Man as strong as you could likely knock down a Texas steer with his bare fist. But I never allowed you had that much temper in you."

Parry said quietly, "I could never abide a man who'd abuse an animal when there's no need. Man like that is the lowest thing that walks." He was silent a moment, rubbing his beard. "You ever hear anyone else in the Basin bad-mouth me, Bill?"

"Nary a one. Folks talk aplenty, sure. But it's always that Will Parry, he's a good neighbor, a damn good man. Don't your ears never burn?"

"You'll sweet-talk me into a raise yet."

"That's what I'm up to." Parry could just make out his grin in the waning starshine. Soholt added, "Virg has got mighty big feet, too."

CHAPTER TWO

NOTHING HAPPENED FOR THE REST OF THE NIGHT, AND nobody was in a fair mood next morning. They had all lost a night's sleep and yet were tense enough not to feel very tired, a poor combination. Few words were passed at the breakfast table where the three hands, as usual, ate with the Parry family. Everyone felt edgy enough to be cautious about showing even a trace of grumpiness. Any cross word might trip off tempers and they were all aware of it.

Right after breakfast, Leah put Ariel and Tim to work sweeping up the broken glass in all the rooms while she made out a shopping list. It was Saturday, which meant town day, and everyone always looked forward to riding in. Today, however, Parry gave orders that nobody was to leave the place. He would go in alone and buy needed supplies and notify Sheriff Kane of last night's doings.

After everyone else had dispersed to their chores, Will and Leah lingered in the kitchen, he pouring a third cup of coffee while she sat at the table and frowned over the list.

"I have a feeling I've left something out. . . ."

Parry turned from the big Monarch stove, cup in hand. "You put down window glass?"

"No." She sighed, tapping her pencil against her teeth. "How much will we need?"

"Too much. I'll figure it out when I get to town." Parry gazed sourly into his cup, thinking of the probable cost,

17

double that if the glass had to be freighted in, and all the damned trouble of installing it so that, like as not, some crazy bastard could knock it all again. "Meantime, we'll need to cover the window holes somehow."

"Oiled paper will do." Leah smiled faintly. "It served us pretty well at one time, didn't it?"

Parry managed to smile back. For most of five years after coming here, they had lived in a rough, mud-chinked, one-room log house that now served as the tack shed. "Yeah. Those were the days."

"When our hearts were young and gay."

"And now they're old and gray."

"You men have a word for that, but I won't say it." Leah laughed, got up, and came around the table and gave him a hug. Even when troubled, she could make a buoyant show of spirits better than the rest of them. "Don't look so hangdog. All in all, we've been pretty lucky. We still are."

Parry set his cup down and put his arms around her, careful as always to nestle the curved side of his hook against her back. He grinned into her hazel eyes, feeling the rounded strength of her body. It was full and almost matronly now, but still well-shaped, and the years had treated her well. Her chestnut hair showed only a sprinkling of gray, and the fine crinkles at the corners of her eyes and full mouth were worn there as much by laughter as by rough living.

Leah had been a Boston debutante whose lovely, slender, and pampered surface had hidden wells of the rock-ribbed strength bequeathed her by Puritan forebears. Though strict enough with the children, she was (thank God) no Puritan. But that inherited iron will had let her defy her monied, Old American family and choose, from a flock of suitors, a husband who was the son of the Irish immigrant who groomed her father's horses.

"Now we must be sober," she said. "What do you really

think, Will? Anything you didn't want to say in front of the children?"

Parry shook his head. "Told you all just what Bill and I talked out. No rhyme or reason to it that we can see. I'll take it to Al Kane, see what he thinks. He's the sheriff; it's his job."

They were still standing close, the deep round hills of her breasts yielding against the pressure of his body but making themselves strongly known. He felt a familiar arousal, and this was no damn time for it. He moved her back from him, hand on her shoulder.

"Maybe what happened last night was all of it. We'll wait it out. Meantime, just see that everyone stays by the place."

"Mm." Leah's eyes sparkled amusedly. "You really want to go to town? To Salvation, I mean?"

"No. But I'm a-goin', ma'am."

He tramped through the back parlor to the front parlor where Ariel and Tim, their youthful spirits already up, were playfully feinting at each other with the brooms instead of sweeping up glass.

"It's a big job," Parry said. "Don't work yourselves to death."

Ariel turned a laughing face to him. All her beautiful red-gold hair was tucked up under the faded blue headcloth she dampened and wore for housework, done up in a cone like a witch's hat.

At fifteen Ariel was as tall as her mother, whom she strongly favored, except for the bright hair she must have gotten from Will's own mother and the eyes as vividly blue as his own, full of the same kindling lights. A tracery of slow-fading freckles lingered across the nose and cheeks of her oval, small-chinned face. Her slim body was still rounding out from the boyishness of preadolescence, but without the gawkiness of many tall girls. Her transition from girl to woman was as graceful as a willow bending in a breeze. *Fifteen!* Ariel looked it and yet, even in a patched calico dress made over from one of her mother's, she struck all of a man's senses with a pure, alive vividness that was nothing but womanly.

God, Parry thought, we'll have to watch her like hawks in another year or so. He wasn't too proud of the thought. She was a wholesome and proper girl for all her high-spiritedness, but lately he'd noticed her playing the coquette a bit with young Truitt Barrows. *Truitt*, for God's sake!

"Daddy"—Ariel tipped her full lips into the cajoling smile with which she always wheedled little favors out of him—"*can't* I go to town? Ma and I were going to shop for dress goods today. She *promised*—"

"It's on the list."

"Oh *Daddy*! What do you know—"

"C'mon, Longlegs!" Tim took a swipe at her with his broom and Ariel jumped back. "All those guys in town today, you just want to make 'em shine up. That's *true*, Pa."

Ariel raised her broom furiously. "You little stink!"

"That's enough, sis. You too, buckshot. You heard what I said before. That's all of it."

Tim grinned disarmingly and said "Aw shise," with no insolence to it, just mildly testing his father, as he began to sweep up glass again. He had Leah's hair and eyes and, at nine, a hint of his father's burliness in his small but solid frame.

Parry glanced at the shelves of worn books on one wall. Quite a few of them were primers, school texts, and copybooks. Because they were ten miles from the nearest schoolhouse, he and Leah had undertaken the kids' education themselves, and they had done a job of it. Leah was a product of Boston's finest finishing schools. Parry, undeterred by his bogtrotter roots and the sparest of schooling in his hard-worked youth, had always been an omnivorous reader, self-taught to read before he was five.

"After you get this mess cleaned up," he told them, "get to the books. Two hours of study. Ariel, I suggest you spend a little more time with higher arithmetic and less with the Romantic poets."

Ariel and Tim gave him looks of genuine distress and said at the same time, "On *Saturday*?"

He grinned at them. "Seems to be one of those days, doesn't it?"

Parry was still grinning as he left the house for the corrals. Leah sometimes scolded him for being too easygoing with the children. Never invoking physical punishment, never raising his voice to them. No need, he would tell her reasonably; results were all that counted. And he'd teased her about never getting over that straitjacket upbringing of hers. Privately, he had to allow that maybe just the formidable look of him kept the kids within subdued limits. It had that effect on most grown men.

Parry paused by the breaking corral where Truitt and Genardo Menocal were working the kinks out of a rough-broken mustang.

"No, no!" the old Mexican was shrilling in his cracked voice. "*Estúpido! Chingado!* How many times I got to tell you, don' pull his head aroun' so goddom far when you ready him to mount!"

Truitt's broad face was red and sweating, and he yelled right back, "My pap learned me all the what-for of cheeking a randy horse, you ol' pepperfart! By God, you . . ."

Parry walked on. Usually he was amused by a raucous exchange between the two, but this morning it held a real acrimony, legacy of the tense night.

He had hired on Truitt Barrows as his new horsebreaker the same day he'd smashed Virg Bollinger's jaw and taken him by wagon to town and Doc Costiner's care. Truitt was only twenty-one and none too bright, but he'd grown up mustanging with his father, a professional horsetrapper, and was already a seasoned horsebreaker; and he had the green bones of youth necessary for the punishing work.

In his time Genardo had been a top *jinete*, a word applied only to the finest of horseworkers. Old, crippled, and embittered, given to grumbling incessantly about anything and everything, he was still second to none when it came to directing the fine points of his craft. Parry had never regretted having taken on Genardo when nobody else in the Basin would give him a job.

At the main corral Parry hitched up the team horses, Rock and Dale, to the spring wagon, climbed to the seat, and put them in motion, swinging toward the ill-defined ruts that served as a road to town. Going past the fir grove beyond the corrals, he reined to a halt as Linc stepped out of the trees.

"You or Bill find any sign yet?" Parry asked.

Linc shoved his old rawhide hat back on his head, combing a hand through the shock of heavy black hair that tumbled over his forehead. "Turned up a few scuff marks on the ground here and there. Enough to show us where he went prowling about is all. Nothing like that one clear print last night. Bill's still poking around on the south side of the place." Linc shook his head. "If he wasn't an Injun, Pa, he was the next thing to it."

"Funny. That's what we always said about you."

Linc flashed his quiet grin.

He was hazel-eyed, taller than his father, but lanky and loosely built to ungainliness, and it wasn't likely he'd fill out much more. Yet he was sure and gliding as a puma in his movements. His moods and thoughts rarely showed, but they darted like quick fish behind his gaunt, taciturn young face. Linc resembled the martyred president who was inaugurated the year before he was born and for whom he was named. Not Lincoln the scholar and aspiring lawyer; rather, Abe the backwoods youth, the rail-splitter. Linc had always tended dutifully to his studies, quietly hating them, and did his chores diligently enough. Meantime he stole every hour he could find to be off ranging the timbered foothills, hunting or fishing or just learning the solitary wilds. Linc had his own nature, his own kind of intelligence, and there was no gain in fighting nature, Parry had often and patiently pointed out to Leah, who loved him and despaired of him.

Parry said, "Don't reckon there's much odds of picking up his trail coming or going."

"Not a lot. One thing, Pa, he came on foot and left the same way. Bill and I have worked out a goodly ways. No fresh horse track anywhere around or near the place."

Parry nodded thoughtfully. This was a land of horsemen where no man, Indian or white, went on foot if he could help it. That would explain the moccasins. A man didn't tackle any kind of distance on foot wearing pinch-toed, high-heeled cowman's boots unless he looked to cripple himself. Afoot and moccasined, too, he'd find it a sight easier to hide his track.

"Keep looking. Need anything from town?"

"Two-three boxes of .44 shells."

Parry smiled and put the wagon forward. Even Leah had to admit it was grand economy to have one offspring like Linc, who worked hard and willingly when he worked, kept the table supplied with game, had no vices at all, and refused any pay but his room and meals, the clothes on his back, and shells for his Winchester. "Don't you worry about that boy," Bill Soholt had told them. "He's as good as a Union greenback. Like enough he'll be getting itchy feet like I did forty years ago and go out in the world and make what he wants of himself."

Parry pulled up at the crown of a broad swell of ground a couple hundred yards east of the layout and looked back at its compact cluster of buildings and corrals and scattered clumps of trees, peaceable and drowsing under the early sun. The big house stood out in high, almost awkward relief beside the low outsheds. It looked extravagant and incongruous in this country where ranch houses were built low and rambling, hugging the ground against summer heat and winter cold, and it was both. But it was the only indulgence Leah had ever asked for and he'd had it built: a two-storied, clapboarded, gabled and dormered New England house half equal in size to the palatial home of her girlhood. It had taken most of five years to build and finish, doling out funds as they could afford to, hiring loggers, sawyers, carpenters to cut and snake the timbers out of the near foothills, shape the beams and planks, and fit the whole thing together. It was worth it. Leah had her New England home and, hoarding what cash she could for the purpose, continued to furnish it to her taste.

Parry drove on, lost in thought. The good times and the bad sort of hazed together in a man's head over the years, a few landmarks of both standing out sharper than others.

He had first set eyes on Chinook Basin in the spring of '61 when, as a twenty-two-year-old deputy sheriff from Jo Daviess County, Illinois, he had been dispatched west to Cheyenne to claim a captured criminal in the charge of U.S. Marshal Alder Kane for special extradition back to Illinois, trial, and punishment. It was Will Parry's first trip to the West, his first meeting with Alder Kane, and his first glimpse of a piece of country he fell in love with on sight.

Leah, whom he had wed two years earlier, had never said so, but he knew she wasn't happy with his lawman's career. And he could hardly wait to tell her that his law days were over, that he had his life's goal set; a small outfit in a beautiful spot on the west slopes of the Wyoming Rockies below the Continental Divide, where they could raise horses and cattle and kids.

But arriving back in Galena, the small Illinois town where he and Leah had settled after eloping from Boston, he knew that the move west would be deferred for a long time. The expected war had erupted, and Ulysses "Sam" Grant, a local ne'er-do-well, was raising a company of militia volunteers. Grant had served in the Mexican War and was good at paperwork. What else he was good at wasn't apparent till the night he rode into camp drunk and fell off his horse. Later, when Grant was appointed colonel of the 21st Illinois Infantry, Will Parry served under him and received a battlefield commission after the fighting at Paducah and Belmont. As one of Grant's favorite officers, Parry had followed his fortunes through the war, from the capture of Forts Henry and Donelson, the retreat from Pittsburgh Landing, the advance on Corinth, and the ferocious and dragged-out siege of Vicksburg, on to victory at Chattanooga, Grant's promotion to head of the army, campaigns at the Wilderness, Cold Harbor, Richmond, and Petersburg, where Will Parry had lost his good right hand to grapeshot.

Another year had passed, recovering from the battlefield amputation and getting his affairs in Illinois settled, before Parry and his family had pulled up stakes and resettled in Wyoming. Looking back, he could see how reckless and ill-considered a move it had been. For him to come completely green into a near-wilderness, a one-handed man almost as green to the horse and cattle trades he wanted to follow, having very limited funds to start with, along with the responsibilities of a wife and two children, one of them a year-old baby, and try settling in just before the high country winter struck, had been little short of lunacy. They'd been lucky not to have been cleaned out after a few months. Lucky, even, to be alive.

Bill Soholt had made the difference, then and through the several years that followed. Bill's seasoned knowledge had provided the touchstone that had saved them from calamity at every crucial turn. Neighbors (the nearest was five miles away) had been kindly, too, helping them get up a cabin that was snug and warm, watching over them that first year, twice bucking deep drifts of snow to sled them grub supplies. Even so, it had been touch-and-go for a long time. And now he had it all, Parry reflected, all he'd wanted and fourteen years of hard, ingrained experience, too.

The country of the Neversummer foothills that enclosed Chinook Basin sprawled in a quiet splendor the year-round, a mixture of plains and dunes mantled with green in spring and early summer, fading to yellow and fawn as the year wore on, then going to a glistening sheet of white. A bent arm of the Neversummers partly sheltered the valley where Parry's WP headquarters lay, isolating it from the upper and lower ranges where most settlers of the Basin had put down their roots. Parry liked that feeling of semi-isolation, but it was a luxury that had its costs and drawbacks.

The land between WP and Salvation was mostly open and rolling, the rough-rutted road skirting low hills formed by remnants of ancient crags that showed here and there, sculptured into weird shapes by time and weather. Scattered groves of pine and juniper grew tough and twisted from the shallow soil. The rich, dew-wet late spring grass was spattered with the pink and blue and lavender of bluebells and larkspur and delphinium. It was a morning made for enjoying, pulling in its fresh savor with all the aliveness of one's senses.

The late morning sun lay bright on the bottomland flats as Parry crossed the heavy bridge over the Blackbow River just below Salvation and rode up its crooked street.

It was an unplanned town, sprawling like a tumble of

children's blocks in a deep crook of the Blackbow. Back after the Mexican War, when the first Anglos had sunk roots in Chinook Basin and begun to build up cattle operations, somebody named Rampant had started a combination trading post/hotel/river ferry at a likely crossing on the Blackbow. Supplies could be freighted there from Cheyenne through Nopal Pass. As the ranches began to flourish on the Basin's rich grasslands, so did the town, hard-drinking and hell-raising. By the early '60s, when a circuit preacher unshipped himself at Rampant's Ferry and announced he was going to raid Hell for a week of nights, the Basin people were enough steeped in settled ways for grumbling but indulgent husbands to let conscientious wives herd them off to meetings. Most of the preacher's conversions stuck no better than a one-two whitewash, but the new name he gave Rampant's Ferry did. Salvation was now a sleepy backwater county seat of wild and little-settled Blackbow County, whose closed mountain ranges were likely to remain that way for a long time.

Parry's first stop was the blacksmith shop, a barnlike, two-storied building with its big double doors standing open. Nils Nansen's forge fire glowed cherry-red in the interior dimness. As Parry swung down from the wagon seat, Nils tramped out to meet him, grinning hugely.

"Will, by *Gud*! You want to try the arm game again?"

Nils was a blond giant of a man whose wide face was boiled ruddy more by the heat of his forge than by open sunlight. He topped Parry by inches and his grimy singlet bared his great-muscled arms. A wooden pegleg showed below his leather apron on his right side. He was as hearty and handsome as you'd expect an old-time Viking corsair to be.

"You couldn't pin me a month back," Parry said. "Maybe you been importing special *lutefisk* from Norway to buck you up."

"Hah! What I been doing, I been trying out a few new twists and tricks. We try it now, *ja*?"

Nils knelt by a big stump near the doorway and plunked his left elbow onto it. Parry knelt opposite him and set his own elbow and they gripped hands. After three straining seconds, Parry wrestled Nils's forearm back and down, pinning it flat to the stumptop.

"Wait . . . wait. *Helvete*, man, I wasn't set! Again."

On the second try Parry pinned Nils's forearm in a second flat.

The big smith rose awkwardly on his foot and peg, chuckling ruefully. "Well, *Gud* damn, I'll never know. I work hard all day with these arms and you got only one you shouldn't put nothing but tallow on, riding a horse the day long working just your ass."

Parry only smiled.

That he was tremendously strong, stronger by far than any man he'd met, was an accepted caprice of nature or heredity. He'd never worked himself harder than any other man in his various occupations. His father had told him that God had imbued a few men of their line, his own father included, with vast strength and just as capriciously had passed over the rest.

Parry said, "Have a look at Rock's right front, will you? The shoe's working loose."

"Fine. Let's have a beer first and talk. I got something to show you on the contraption."

"Later. I have to see Al Kane."

"*Ja?* What's more important than the contraption?"

Parry told him about last night.

Nils Nansen rubbed the back of his neck, frowning. "Well, now there's a caution. *Ja*, Virg Bollinger is still around. Drifted back a couple weeks ago in company with three others, saddle bummers the lot."

"Others?"

"*Ja*, three. Al has got their sign plain as rain, don't you fret none. You talk to him." Nils's broad face brightened. "Listen, Will, the contraption—I got a new design worked up. When I show you, by *Gud*! I tell you, we get it rigged on, you'll be shooting a rifle again. Good as ever!"

Parry angled through the tumbled-block sprawl of Salvation's streets toward the north end of town, smiling to himself. Big Nils was half scientist and half boy in his enthusiasms. He was an intent and constant analyst of his own craft, sure that intricate and useful miracles could be wrought in iron if a man found the right key. Like Emerson, who couldn't have invented anything to save his life, Nils believed that if a man could invent a better mousetrap, the world would beat a path to his door. And he did have a knack for devising small gadgets of doubtful value, like an automatic chicken feeder that worked okay but was far more trouble to rig up for use than it was worth. Nils's latest brainstorm was a dingus that Parry could strap on his arm stump in place of a mere hook. The dingus had slots and clamps and brackets of various kinds into which, theoretically, a man could fit a tool for any task a two-handed man might perform. Anything from a knife or fork to a hammer or saw. Or even an attachment that would enable him to grip and aim and fire a rifle. That his first three versions had turned out to be as unworkable as teats on a boar hadn't dampened Nils Nansen's optimism by a drop.

The Nopal County Courthouse was a two-story, Corinthian-columned brick building set on a stretch of pleasant lawn that was kept in raggedly short trim by a special mower Nils had invented. Parry cut around to a side door that was plainly lettered SHERIFF'S OFFICE and let himself in.

Alder Kane was seated at a swivel chair by a rolltop desk.

As Parry entered, he rose stiffly and extended a thin, veined hand, saying mildly, "How, boy."

Standing, Kane was an unusually tall man, stoop-shouldered and so gauntly built he seemed almost cadaverous. His face was long and mournful, his slightly protuberant eyes were palest blue, and his handlebar mustache had turned pure white, giving him almost a theatrical look. So, in an odd way, did the respectable broadcloth suit he wore, its dead blackness relieved only by the dull gleam of a sheriff's star on his vest. But a man would be wise not to ignore the penetrating quality of those eyes or the square thrust of Kane's jaw in his long face. He was old, in his upper sixties now, but the years hadn't eroded either his wits or his perceptions. He served both as county sheriff and Salvation's town marshal, and no resident of the Basin had any doubts of his ability to handle both jobs. Alder Kane had been one of the most respected lawmen in the West, a United States marshal for many years, until age had forced his retirement to this quiet backwater.

"Haven't seen you in a good while, Will. What's the trouble?"

"That plain?"

Alder Kane nodded. "You ain't a man shows much. But it's there. I can see it. Don't ask me how. You get an eye for it."

Parry slacked into a vacant chair. He told Kane about the trouble.

"You think Bollinger, eh?"

Parry lifted his shoulders in a spare shrug. "No way of saying. Virg has big feet. He's handy with a rifle. He knows my place, the whole layout. He's a handy woodsman and he always moved like one. None of that's proof. But he's the only one in these parts likely to bear me a grudge."

"Yeah." Kane picked up a pencil from his desk and

stroked his jaw with it. "He made some high-rolling talk against you, too. That's no proof either."

"Al, it's the best I can give you. If last night was all of it, I'd say let it be. But I don't think it was."

Kane nodded morosely. "There's Little Crow's bunch. But you reckon that's an outside possibility."

"Don't you?"

Kane sighed and pitched the pencil into a litter of papers. "Yeah. Little Crow's bunch is camped a ways up the Blackbow. I'll drop out and see him. Smoke and make talk. I don't look to learn much, but I'll hazard if Crow finds any of his boys was at fault, they'll catch hot hell. If it was Virg and his friends, now . . ."

"It was just one man last night, Al." Parry paused. "Who are these 'friends' of his? Saddle bums, Nils said."

"Just some cronies he picked up in his drifting," Alder Kane said. "You were a U.S. deputy marshal for a time back in, what was it, Galena. You must have got an eye for the breed. They're all over the country since the crash of '73. Bums, 'boes and bindle stiffs. Gang up, work a little, steal some, ride the rails, mostly just drift."

"Never got too many of those out my way."

"Same out here as anywhere, 'cept they go horseback if they got horses, ride a grubline. And they're liable to be tough nuts, handy with guns, knives. Some of 'em have wanted flyers on 'em somewheres if I trouble to check. More bother'n it's worth to come down on 'em. Make trouble here, I put the run on 'em, unless it's something serious."

"No ruckus-raising by Virg or his pals?"

"Not yet. They buck the tiger every night one place or another, but no bellystripping I heard tell of. Drink a lot and noise it up. Turn enough money at the tables to keep 'emselves in grub and booze and even a little roosterin' over at Horrid Hattie's fancy house. Nothing rough, though. I don't put the run on a man for anything less."

Parry was silent a moment, weighing his thoughts. "At least I can have a talk with Virg."

"Both of us can. Him and his friends have made 'emselves a 'jungle' up the river a piece. Just a piddlin' walk. I'll show you."

CHAPTER THREE

PARRY AND KANE LEFT THE COURTHOUSE AND SWUNG
north out of town. The dim trace of an old Indian trail ran
along the west bank of the river, and they followed it.
Sunlight danced in silvery scallops on the amber stretch of
the Blackbow as it brawled down toward the lowlands past
Salvation. A spring lacework of pale green willow foliage
mantled the banks; curlews swooped and sounded across the
water. It was pleasant to idle along the trail and just talk,
and they came almost suddenly on the "jungle" or tramp
camp.

Crossing a high arch of ground above the riverbank, they
smelled fresh coffee and heard men's voices ahead, a
grumbling one, a rowdy and laughing one, and both
punctuated by plenty of swearing. Then they topped the rise
and looked down at the camp. It was on a low tongue of
land that projected into the river, a wide and open space
hemmed around by a loose cordon of rocks and willow
brush. Still a favorite campsite of the Indians because winds
passing over the point kept insect pests to a minimum, it had
a pleasant seclusion about it that even its present disorder
couldn't cancel out. Saddles, blankets, clothing, utensils,
odd pieces of camp gear were scattered carelessly around.
Four horses were hobbled out on a stretch of grass. A ring
of blackened stones contained a low fire. A man squatted on
his heels beside it, turning bacon in a skillet.

Virg Bollinger was sprawled on an old army blanket, head propped on his saddle, a bottle tilted to his lips. Wearing only his grimy red long johns and socks and a battered Stetson, he was the image of slovenly comfort. As Parry and Kane came down off the rise, he turned his head, his scruffy reddish beard still parted as he slugged from the bottle, Adam's apple bobbing in his thick neck.

Virg lowered the bottle. "Boys, howdy. Seems Jesus loves us after all. We got sent a pair of redeemers. Holier'n Hell Parry and Raisin' Kane, yep, raisin' the sinners to glory."

Hard to tell about Bollinger's state of mind except that he was quietly drunk. Working for Parry, he'd been that way a lot of the time without it affecting his horseworking skills. He might be jocular, he might be tranquil, he might be seething mean just under the surface. And his temper, Parry remembered, could be volatile and fast-breaking and uncontrollable.

"That's Parry for sure?" one of Virg's cronies said with interest. He was a stringy-looking man in his fifties, gnarled and grizzled. "One you say busted your jaw?"

"That's the bastard, Joe."

Kane turned his head a little, letting his palefrost stare settle on the grizzled man. "Joe Million," he said mildly. "Wanted for stealing a horse at Leavenworth, Kansas, where the warrant was made out. That was four years ago, but it never got served that I know of."

Virg and his friends exchanged looks. They all knew of Kane's old reputation, who didn't, but likely had him pegged for an aged, tank town has-been.

"What's 'at to you, Gran'paw?" asked the one who was frying bacon. He was a gangling weed of a youth and about the dirtiest of the four, his clothes ingrained with grease and dirt and old sweat.

"Nothing just yet, Chunk," Kane said. "Robert 'Chunk' Fetterson, ain't it? Your daddy was killed riding with

Quantrill and Bloody Bill Anderson. Think a bright lad like you 'ud take a lesson. But you never did. Took up with one of your daddy's old running mates, Jesse 'Dingus' James, and got spotted on a job with him. Only one witness, and he got dusted off somehow a little later on. Convenient, that."

Chunk Fetterson dumped the bacon in the fire and got to his feet. "Anything else, Gran'paw?"

"Outside of you spoiled a mess of bacon, no."

"Hey, Pop. What about me?"

The fourth man was lounging against a big rock on Kane's far right. He was fooling with his revolver, idly spilling out the cartridges in his palm and fitting them back in the chambers. He was very dark with black stringy hair, some Indian blood and a zigzag slash scar that laid his face pinkly open on one side. "I'm Pony Teal. You know anythin' 'bout me?"

"Two things for sure," Kane said. "I can smell you upwind and you look nervous with a gun. Rest is hearsay. You got sent to Yuma Prison for peddling whiskey to old Loco just before him and his braves busted off San Carlos Reservation. That was five years ago and you pulled five years. You must be fresh out."

Pony Teal jerked out a chuckle and looked at Virg. "Old fart still keeps his pecker up, don't he? Knows his bad men pretty well."

"He's s'posed to. It's his job." Virg hadn't once taken his eyes off Parry. Now he drained the bottle, sailed it against a rock and climbed to his feet.

Bollinger was in his mid-twenties, not at all rangy and wiry as you'd expect a bronc-peeler to be. He was squarely built, heavy and solid; he looked as strong as a bull and was. But he also had catlike reflexes you wouldn't suspect till you'd seen him in action. Nobody, Parry guessed, had ever laid Virg in the dust before he did. Likely Virg still only half-believed it. So far his muddy stare held more of a curious perplexity than of smoldering rancor.

"You got business with us, Mr. Kane?"

"Depends," Kane said. "Someone shot up Mr. Parry's place last night. They killed all the chickens in his coop and busted all the windows in his house."

Virg's beard parted again. This time he was forming a grin. It showed a gap of three missing upper teeth. "Yeah? Any idea who done it?"

"Prime question. Thought we'd put it to you."

"Boy, do I wish I knew. I'd buy the man a drink." Virg laughed and threw out his hands expansively. "Don't know if I know him, but I sure's hell don't know what he was doing last night. That's 'cause I was here all night last night. All of us was."

"Damn well told," Joe Million said. "All of us."

All four were watching Parry and Kane in a measuring, guarded way, the way of men who'd had their bad brushes with regulated society and held a mean-cur suspicion of it. Hard to gauge their collective temper, because each would be juggling a collection of private hostilities in his head. None was really drunk, except maybe for Virg, but each looked as if he'd put down a few swallows of dog's hair on a bad hangover.

"Then," Kane said easily, "you could give each other alibis if I was inclined to ask you for 'em."

"That's right," Bollinger said. "You asking?"

"Virg, you passed some damn mean talk against Will Parry. From what's been told me, it sounded like killing talk."

"Likker talk," Bollinger said blandly. "You don't lay no stock by that, do you?"

Kane watched him unblinkingly. Bollinger laughed. "Man's free to talk plain out. Say any damn thing he wants. I know that much law. It's doin' that counts."

"That's right."

"And you got to have evidence for doin'. Now don't you, sir?"

Kane's glance circled, touching on the guns in the camp. Only Fetterson and Teal were armed at the moment, both with six-guns, but pistols and rifles poked out of the scattered gear.

"You boys are pretty well-heeled. Mind showing me all your guns?"

"Hell yes we mind," Virg said, grinning. "You got anything you can pull us in for, do it. Otherwise get the hell out of here."

"After we've had a look at your guns," Parry murmured. "I'm looking for the one that shot up my place. Offhand, I'd say it was a Winchester lever-action carbine, model '73 or '76."

Bollinger shaped a faint grin, but his bloodshot eyes heated with a mounting anger. "I got one. '76. You want to see it?"

"And smell it. Find if it burned a lot of powder in the last few hours."

"Sure," Bollinger said. He walked over to a rock and picked up a carbine leaning against it, then tramped slowly toward Parry till he stood less than ten feet away. "Do better'n that. I'll feed it down your fucking gullet butt first. Or you want to turn around and start walking?"

Parry said quietly. "You better sing soft, Virg."

"My jaw's all healed," grinned Bollinger. "I reckon it'll keep that way. Had my back turned to you just before you coldcocked me. I come around fast and you busted me before I was set. Done some figuring on that. What I figure, you had a rock, something like that, in your hand."

"Virg, you were drunk enough not to be sure if you got hit by a rock or a mule's hind leg. All that hit you was me."

"Like hell," Bollinger said softly. He tossed the carbine aside. His eyes were reddening to slits of pure rage. "We'll do that waltz again. Only this time around I got your number. Go ahead. Throw one at me."

Parry shook his head impatiently. "I didn't come to brace you. Just—"

"That little girl of yours," Bollinger said gently, wickedly. "She growed up any more since I last—"

"You better drop it right there." Parry's voice was as rip-edged as a saw, cutting across Bollinger's.

"Man, she was coming up fine as froghair. Nice little jugs on 'er and I don't know what-all. I would sure admire to see—"

Parry was already moving in on him, fast and with an unthinking fury. Virg was fast too, weaving back and sideways in a jerky dance step, almost avoiding Parry's swing. But not quite. Parry's fist glanced off his temple with only a skidding impact, but it was enough to send Bollinger staggering. He tripped and fell on his back.

"Get up," Parry said thickly.

"Will, go easy."

Kane's voice came sharp and warning at Parry's back, but he hardly heard it. He watched Bollinger get one knee under him and ease to his feet, his stance wary. And the other three were coming alert now, shifting their feet. Parry knew in that moment that he might be taking on more than just Virg.

Kane pushed the skirt of his coat back from his holstered gun, saying flatly, "You men stay clear."

"Who's going to make us, Pop?" asked Pony Teal. His idly held gun was suddenly trained on Kane. "You stay set now."

Chunk Fetterson walked over to Kane and took the sheriff's gun from its holster and stepped back. "Gran'paw's tooth been pulled, Virg. You go at it, now. You don't need to do it under no gun."

Bollinger's teeth were bared. He rubbed the flat of his hand over his temple. Then he bored in at Parry, feinting at his middle and throwing a stiff right at his jaw.

Parry slipped most of the blow by turning his head, but it rocked his jaw like a club all the same. He accepted its force, not rolling with the punch, to get Virg inside his reach. He balled up a fistful of Virg's underwear, half-swung him from his feet, and flung him away. Bollinger slammed the ground on his side, rolled over twice, and landed in the fire.

He scrambled out of it with a howl, batting at live embers that clung to his smoldering underwear. He shook his head like a bull and then, his eyes crazed, grabbed up his fallen rifle and lunged at Parry. There was no thought in his mind of firing the weapon, no room for anything but the feral urge to strike and smash. He was pure animal in his rage, and now Parry's own anger was clearing away.

Virg swung the rifle back two-handed above his head, grasping the barrel, and took a powerful swing at Parry's skull. Parry let the stock smack against his upflung palm. He closed his fist around it and gave one savage wrench that threw Virg off balance, twisting the rifle from his grasp. Parry swung the rifle backward and forward and let go, sending it out in a high sun-winking arc, end over end, over the river. It hit the swift current with a thready splash and was gone.

Bollinger backed off with a gusty snort, fear in his eyes now. Sobered by the hard swiftness of Parry's reactions, he could realize the mistake he'd made. He'd set himself against a man of killing strength, a man deliberately containing that strength, and now he knew it.

"Will!"

The flat warning word came from Kane. From the corner of his eye Parry saw Joe Million coming at his side and back, and he pivoted fast on his heel. Sun raced along the steel flash of a blade as Million stopped in his lunge, snapping the weapon out of a boot sheath. It was an Arkansas toothpick, the frontier dagger, a blade designed for fighting and killing and nothing else.

Million's grizzled jaw was set, his eyes snake-cold with an old and deadly wisdom. He moved in a knifefighter's crouch, knife hand a little extended, left hand palm out as a guard. And then he thrust, a straight-armed stab aimed at Parry's right side, high enough to sever underarm muscles and disable, not kill. If it found the mark, severing nerves and muscle fiber clean and quick, a man would never use that arm again.

Parry might think of that later, now he only instinctively side-shifted and raised suddenly on his toes. Just a few inches and with a spareness of motion, enough to let the blade pass between his trunk and his hook arm, not quite grazing flesh. Forward on the balls of his feet, off balance, Million caught himself and tried to step back. But his forearm was suddenly clamped between Parry's side and arm.

Parry's left hand came up, the callused heel of his palm sledging into Million's jaw with a force that snapped his head back. Million's eyes washed to blankness as he went limp, sagging down. Parry lifted his arm, unlocking Million's, and let him fall.

The sheriff shouted again, but Parry was already aware of Virg plowing at him once more, just as Chunk Fetterson moved in on his other side, both trying to seize the instant's advantage. Chunk had his six-gun out, lifted to chop at Parry's head.

Parry didn't turn toward either man. He simply swung his hook arm in a full arc that slammed the steel curve of the hook against Chunk's forehead. Chunk gave a shriek of pain and surprise and stopped in his tracks, dropping his gun, clapping both hands to his head. Blood spurted between his fingers.

Parry was already turning to face Virg and this time he put all his strength into his swing. Only the back of his fist struck Bollinger, but it was enough to send him kiting head over heels. Virg landed facedown and lay groaning.

Parry tramped over to him and bent, snagging his hook in a fold of Virg's baggy underwear and hauling him half-upright.

"Leave go of him!" Pony Teal yelled. "Leave go, you hear?"

His voice was panicky and now his pistol was pointed at Parry, not at Kane.

That froze the situation, but the outcome was already clear. Million was laid out cold; Fetterson was pawing at his streaming forehead and wildly crying that, Christ, he was blind, his goddam eyes were burning up (from a briny sting of blood in them); and Virg was sprawled and feebly stirring, but gasping in real pain.

I must have broken his jaw again, Parry thought. It felt like it.

Alder Kane had waited for the right moment and this was it. He hiked his bony shoulders high under his black suit and started walking slowly toward Pony Teal, saying quietly, "I'll take that hogleg, son."

"Like hell you will, Pop!" Teal's face had a wild vicious set in the matted frame of his stringy hair. "You goddam stop right there!"

Kane kept walking. "Turn it in your hand," he said in an implacable voice. "Hold it out butt first."

"Stuff it up your jiggy, Pop!"

Teal cocked the pistol.

Kane's steady stride never faltered and he kept talking, saying quietly, "Pull the trigger and I'm maybe dead. But you're dead for sure. Or worse. If I die, you'll swing for it. If I live, I'll see your ass buried in territorial prison so deep down you won't see daylight for twenty years. Remember Yuma, Pony? Remember the snake pit? They ever drop you in the—"

Pony Teal let out a frustrated whoop and, in his moment of booze-blurred indecision, jerked the trigger. But Kane

was already square in front of him, his hand coming down
on the gun and closing around the frame. There was no snap
of hammer, no shot fired. Parry heard Kane's grunt of pain
and saw him disarm Pony Teal with one quick twist.

Now Kane held the gun, but blood was pouring off his
hand. He squinted, grimacing, as he stepped away from
Teal and thumbed back the hammer with his free hand.
Parry saw what Kane had done: jammed his hand down so
that when the hammer fell, the firing pin had embedded
itself in the web of skin between thumb and forefinger.

Parry's anger was wholly gone now, but he'd begun a
final piece of business and disliked leaving it unfinished.
Having hook-hauled Bollinger to his knees, his head lolling
sideways, Parry reached down and grabbed him by the leg,
too, and carried him to the riverbank. He freed the hook and
then, one-armed, pitched Virg into the water.

Bollinger tumbled with the current a few yards, getting
ducked twice. He floundered to his feet and over to the
bank, dropping to his hands and knees, coughing and
gagging on the water he'd swallowed. His freshly broken
jaw made it plain agony.

"Next time your face is fixed," Parry told him meagerly,
"careful how you shoot it off."

Kane was collecting all the weapons, dropping them in a
single pile. Afterward he wrapped a bandanna around his
bleeding hand while Parry went over the rifles, examining
each one. There were two army Springfields and two recent-
model Winchester repeaters. Virg's stank of burned powder,
but so did the others. None looked as if they'd been
properly cleaned after some recent heavy use.

"We done some target shooting yestiday," Pony Teal said
sullenly. "That's all. There's a lot a shot-up tin cans back in
the rocks yonder. Look for y'selves."

Parry didn't bother. He rummaged through Virg's possi-
bles looking for something else: a pair of Cheyenne

moccasins. He found only a pair of runover boots. What the hell did that mean? Only that Virg might have worn moccasins last night and cached them elsewhere.

Million, sitting on the ground and nursing his own sore head, looked irritably at Chunk, who was still whining about the two-inch split in the skin of his forehead. "Quit bellyachin'. I'll sew that up for you directly," His hard glance shifted to Kane. "You of a mind to haul us in now?"

"For a piddlin' trifle," Kane said, "why bother? All you'd do is get room and board free on the county till you was let out. Then you'd go on hanging about till you took a mind to drift or I had to jug you for something else. I'll save you the trouble. You pack up now. Start riding south. That's the nearest way to the county line. Be across it by this time tomorrow. Any of you shows himself back here again, I'll run him off the hard way. Got all that? You got it, Virg?"

Bollinger climbed painfully to his feet, cuddling his lopsided jaw in one palm, his eyes squinched with pain. "Yeah," he said in an awkward mumble, using only his tongue. "We going now. Only—" His bloodshot gaze shuttled to Parry. "I didn' mean nothin' I said before. Now I do. I gonna nail you, old boss. I gonna nail your balls to a shithouse wall 'fore I done. You bank on it. . . ."

Parry and Kane left the camp, tramping back toward town. They were nearly to the outskirts when Kane broke the silence, saying mildly, "They're a triflin' crew, Will. They'll drift. Except Virg, maybe. Only if he comes back, he'll sneak back. That's how I read him. You watch yourself, hear?"

Parry barely nodded. He had a baffled, unsettling conviction that the threat against him or his ran deeper than he knew. And he couldn't account for the feeling.

CHAPTER FOUR

WEATHER IN THE HIGH COUNTRY COULD TURN ITSELF UPSIDE down overnight. Snow might clog the high passes and iron cold grip the land; you'd go to bed one night with the fatalistic knowledge that you were frozen up and snowed in till spring. And within hours you'd wake up to the roar of a chinook, a warm thaw wind that had the eaves dripping and the drifts speedily shrinking. Just as suddenly the process could reverse itself. Even in late spring, with new grass greening the high pastures, buds bursting, and early wildflowers poking out, the weather could do an about-face and show savage fangs.

Yesterday, when Will Parry and his sons had set out on their horse hunt, it had been fair and warm all day and into the early dark as they set up camp high in the Buckhorn Hills. Snow fell in the night, skittering down in big, globby flakes that quickly melted on the warm earth. By dawn the soil was frozen and whistling blasts of hard, stinging snow were pelting their prone forms, silvering the creases of their Mackinaw coats and blankets, making them shiver in the rock-sheltered covert where they'd bivouacked. They didn't get much sleep, and morning dawned gray and raw with thin powder snow still raking along the cutting wind.

Will and Linc and Tim huddled around their sheltered fire, wolfing cold sandwiches made of supper leftovers, holding them awkwardly in their mittened hands, as they watched coffee come to a boil over the wind-tattered flames.

"Pa, it's a day for white owls," Linc said. "Maybe we best turn back and try again in a week or so."

Parry shook his head. "Little Crow's man said they spotted Soldado and his bunch on the Washoe Bench two days ago. We wait a week, the herd might be miles from there. Soon as the passes open up come spring, those horses get on the move."

Linc only nodded. He'd raised the suggestion solely for Tim's sake, Parry knew. Tim had worn him ragged, wheedling to be taken along on this horse hunt, his first. Hunkered now by a fire that hardly warmed, the boy was chilled and unhappy, his nine-year-old spirits dragging rock bottom. But he'd begged onto this job against all Parry's warnings about what a misery it could turn into. If a boy bought into a man's business, he was obliged to ride it out like a man.

So far Tim hadn't voiced a word of complaint. When Linc poured the coffee, Tim drank it black and steaming hot like his father and brother, nursing his hands around the tin cup when it had cooled enough, holding a bleak and stubborn silence. Parry grinned to himself, knowing just how the boy felt: mad and miserable, not far short of tears maybe, but determined to tough it out. And he would.

The three of them had gone out for a few days of scouting the back country to the northwest where the Buckhorns came up against the lower slopes of the Neversummer Range. One of Little Crow's Cheyennes had brought Little Crow's good friend Parry word that Old Soldado, the wild herding stallion who had sometimes raided Parry's stable pasture for mares, had returned from the deep valleys of the Neversummers where he wintered. Apparently his herd of mares and younglings had almost been wiped out during this particularly long and fierce winter. Now Soldado was looking to replenish his harem from Chinook Basin stock and, as always, Parry's WP spread was a favorite target of his.

The Cheyennes had spotted several of Parry's horses in Soldado's band, also a half-dozen wild mares he must have found upcountry. It would be worth a several days' hunt if the Parrys could recover their own stock and round up a few additional wildlings for breaking and trading.

More than on his small herd of purebred Herefords, Parry depended on his mustanging and horse raising and trading to secure a comfortable living for his family. Troops quartered at Fort Sanford on the big Ute reservation had a regular need for cavalry re-mounts and he could sell all that he raised, as well as the wild mustangs he and his crew caught and rough-broke and gentled, provided their basic specifications and conformations, their soundness of wind and limb, met the exacting standards of the army vets and line officers. The U.S. Cavalry wanted only the best horseflesh; Will Parry supplied them with the best and was well paid for it.

Briefly, Parry's thoughts ranged back to his encounter with Virg Bollinger and his friends three days ago. Would there be more trouble from that quarter?

Hard to say. Rough-treating some men might throw the fear of God into them. But a man of Virg's stripe? Good chance that Alder Kane was right. Stubborn, vicious, grudge-holding, Bollinger might try a reprisal of some sort. *If* he was the one behind the trouble. And even if he wasn't . . . he'd now have more reason than ever to hate Will Parry's guts. You did what you had to, Parry told himself, but it was thin comfort.

Anyway, he'd renewed his warning to his wife, his daughter, and his crewmen. Soholt and Truitt and Genardo had orders to confine themselves to duties that would keep them close to WP headquarters and they were to go armed at all times. Leah and Ariel had guns at hand in the house.

Danger, as much as hardship, was a possibility you

learned to live with day by day in this country. You couldn't just sit about on your butt waiting and worrying about what *might* happen. You never knew for sure. The business of everyday living still had to be attended to. Best to push worry as much out of mind as you could and get on with the job.

Parry swigged the last of his coffee and said, "Let's be going, boys."

The three assembled their gear. The saddle mounts and packhorse were hobbled nearby in a deep fissure, the walls of which broke the slashing gusts of wind and snow. They diamond-hitched their tarp-covered gear on the packhorse and saddled up.

"We pretty well covered the south bench yesterday, Pa," said Linc. "If we don't scare up sign of ol' Soldado and his herd on the north bench today, it's likely been a bum trip."

Parry nodded. "In that case we'll head for home. But I want to be sure. Lead out, son."

They fell into their usual pattern of march, Linc moving well into the lead so that his woodscraft would ferret out anything unusual on the immediate or faraway terrain, something that might take alarm if someone less keenly alert than he were to blunder onto it. And Linc would spot any close-up ground sign, track that another man on horseback might carelessly obliterate before he knew it.

The Washoe Bench was so called because it formed a kind of high plateau between the Buckhorn Hills and the Neversummers to the northeast. But it wasn't a regular tableland as its name suggested. Its surface was chopped into serrated badlands, wild and broken, which had become a refuge for roving bands of wild mustangs after the white man's encroachments had driven them out of the lower basin. Making a detailed search of its maze of shouldering ridges and cross-hatching canyons, its scattered pine parks and crazy quilt patches of meadow, would take days.

Generally Will and his sons stuck to the high ground wherever they could, trying to absorb the terrain in a general scrutiny. Even so, it was slow work; the rugged going held them to a snail's pace.

This morning they worked steadily north in a zigzag pattern that took them northeast and then northwest and back again. Both Will and Linc had high-powered glasses and they stopped often to use them, searching the landscape far and near, hampered by obstructions of all kinds. It was frustrating to know that you could be conning only the rimrock of a near canyon that was deep and wide enough to hide hundreds of horses and not be sure. But that was the horsehunting game. Anything from a failed outing to a grand catch might hinge on pure luck.

It was getting harder as the years went by to make the trade worthwhile. The itinerant mustangers would clean out a piece of country and move on and not return unless its mustang population grew back. The wildlings that remained would grow more wary, less easy to trap, and a man had to range farther to pick them up.

Parry and Linc knew the country. So did old Genardo Menocal, but his riding days were over. Genardo's good use lay in his training methods, his uncanny way with horseflesh. With Truitt Barrows to handle the rough-breaking—for which Parry was too old and Linc had no inclination—they made a good team all around. Young Tim already held a fine seat on a horse; about the time Truitt was edging out of his early twenties and could no longer handle the rough work, Tim might take over. . . .

Linc's sharp "Pa!" broke Parry's idle musing. Linc had halted on the brink of a dip where the land fell away in easy undulations. There was dense timber in the near distance and belts of winter-withered meadow barely starting to green out.

Linc pointed. "Right there . . . to the left of that needle rock. "See 'em?"

A pocket of humpy meadow slanted off from the rock, and halfway across it Parry saw ten horses. He knew several of them. A young mare that Soldado had driven off his stable pasture a couple of weeks back and a placid gray gelding who had trailed them. A blaze-faced sorrel mare that a neighbor had lost a year back. A clutch of wildlings that included three mares and their foals. And there was old Soldado himself, still proud and powerful in his late prime, his dappled white coat almost invisible behind the thin veil of swirling snow. He'd come through a terrible winter in good shape, as you'd expect of him.

Parry lowered the glasses, a faint smile on his lips. Over the years he'd come to a kind of loving admiration of the old devil. Twice in the past, in situations where he might have been able to maneuver Soldado into a trap, he'd made only half-hearted efforts to do so. Fact was, he felt that if the big stallion was ever captured or killed, his free spirit broken forever, something would go out of Will Parry, too—out of the deepest meaning this country and its remaining wilderness held for him.

All the same he'd try to run Soldado to ground himself if he could, or somebody else would fetch him dead before long. Soldado was a wild herding stallion. He'd become a sworn target of ranchers who were tired of having their best breeding stock trailed off.

Parry didn't want to contemplate that eventuality just now. But he did want to recover the kidnapped stock and, if possible, entrap those wild ones and their younglings, too.

Linc, as if reading his thoughts, said, "Pa, we work around east of 'em, we might be able to walk 'em down. There's that pen we built over against Ganlon Bluff three years ago. If she's still in passable shape, we can work 'em in there slick as a whistle. Maybe."

"Right. Let's have a look at it."

They descended the short dip and struck north and east

toward Ganlon Bluff. The pen Linc had referred to was practically a natural trap, a vast U-shaped hollow in the bluffside forming three of its curving walls. They had built a hundred-foot fence across the fourth, open side, sinking pairs of posts two feet apart, lashing them together with rawhide, and packing limbs and brush between them. The fence was taller than any horse could jump and invincible to any that might try to crash through.

For all their labor in getting the corral rigged, they'd never succeeded in driving a *caballada* of wild ones into it. Either they would try to haze a bunch too far and the animals would get skittish enough to break away from their would-be captors or the terrain itself, rugged with odd turns and twists of ancient trails, would cause the horses to jitter off in wrong directions. But the present location of Soldado and his band—not far from the bluff and close to the broad end of a funnel-shaped canyon that led almost to the pen along a narrowing trail—meant that if they got them pointed into the wide rim of the funnel the horses wouldn't realize in time that they were being pinched into a trap.

The big problem would be to get them headed the right way at the outset.

Parry and his sons found the post-and-brush fence intact, as secure as they'd last seen it a year ago. They rode along it, tugging at the rawhide lashings, finding them unrotted and intact. The fence had been constructed so that it formed two giant wings extending out to the tip of the canyon funnel where double gates were hung. When the gates were swung wide open they touched the canyon walls on either side and formed a kind of chute. A bunch of horses being driven down the funnel stem would have no choice but to enter it. From there they'd plunge unknowingly into the big enclosed trap. Working quickly, the horsehunters could drag the double gates shut and secure them. A surpassingly easy way to snare horses. And nature itself had provided nearly all the construction work.

All they had to do to set the trap was drag the unwieldy gates to wide open position. Hinged with still-flexible rawhide straps, they were heavy and difficult to budge; the underedges scraped ground and the gates virtually had to be lifted clear as they were swung wide. Parry's great strength was taxed to move each one: getting both closed in time, he'd need every iota of muscle his sons could add to his own.

But they could manage it, he was sure. Once they had the animals in the trap, they could manage.

As they rode back up the canyon, Parry worried that the swirl of wind-slanting snow might undo everything. It was too light to impede visibility; it coated the ground in fine drifting streamers that wouldn't slow the horses. But once they were out of the canyon, a worsening mixture of driving wind and biting snow laced against their exposed skin; its iron chill cut to the bone. They tied scarves around their lower faces and over their hats to hold them in place, turned up their collars, and huddled deeper into their Mackinaw coats.

To skirt wide of Soldado's bunch and get around back of it they began a slow and circuitous crossing of the rugged benchland, keeping always out of view of the band. They made their swing south of it to stay downwind. Blowing snow lashed their faces and left sides. Their eyes watered and the tears froze on their cheeks. At this slow pace, even protected by sheepskin mitts, their fingers grew numb around the reins. They curled their toes in their boots and worked them constantly against frostbite.

Parry pulled up at last. The leather of his rig creaked with cold as he swung around to study the lay of the land, turrets of gray rocks and spindles of dark pine against a drab sky. A rough horseshoe of small hills almost surrounded the flats where the mustangs were. The hills were bisected by clefts so that the three Parrys could split up and fan out back of the hills, unseen till they rode through the clefts onto the flat. Then they'd simultaneously approach the band from three sides, hazing Soldado and his harem gently into motion on an eastward line. And walk them into the trap.

Parry explained it to them. Linc hardly needed telling, but Parry laid it out carefully for Tim's sake, stressing that he must watch his flanks as well as his front, keeping aware of his father's and brother's movements so they'd all maintain an even pace as they closed in.

Tim blinked against the skittering bite of flakes. The wind flapped his hatbrim up and down. "Okay, Pa. But jeez. This wind is something."

"It sure is, buckshot. If it's too much for you, now's the time to say so. We'll plunk you down in these rocks out of the wind and do it by ourselves."

"I didn't say nothing about quitting!"

Tim's words came muffled and outraged through his face scarf; his wet, reddened eyes blinked angrily. Parry nodded. Linc gave his brother a solemn wink, saying, "You take it easy now, buckshot."

Parry swung his arm. "Linc, you come around that side. Tim, you take it from the other. I'll push straight in behind 'em. Slow and easy does it. No sudden moves, even if they start to break direction. If they do, crowd 'em back into line easy. If you can. If you can't, if they break away fast, let 'em go. Don't take any fool chances, understand?"

They split apart now and Parry sat his mount, watching his sons ride out of sight. He'd assigned Tim to the side where, for a time at least, he'd have the bitter wind at his back.

Leah had voiced worry about his taking the boy along on this job. In mildly reassuring her, Parry had hidden his own concern. This was man's work for sure. The country demanded early manhood of a boy, but you worried about every step of the initiation. Tim was a year younger than Linc had been on his first horsehunt. Still, except for the savage discomfort of the job—heightened by an unexpected turn of weather—it shouldn't hold any real danger.

When he judged the time was right, Parry put his mount forward through the nearest cleft, holding him and the packhorse tied behind to a walk. They emerged onto a flat snowfield the surface of which was already crisping under the subzero wind. The horse's hoofs broke the shallow crust at each step. Linc and Tim were coming into sight on Parry's left and right, dark moving shapes through the blasts of snow. The three of them converged gradually on the bunch of horses standing in a protective circle, rumps outward.

Gradually now the bunch broke apart. Soldado snorted and wheeled away, leading east. He moved unhurriedly, with a wary confidence. He'd eluded many a horsetrapper and would expect easily to do so again, even if he lost a few of his band. The other animals trailed him, not terribly spooked. They were all familiar with humans, and only the wildlings were likely to bolt.

The Parrys followed slowly, edging a little nearer all the time, keeping the rear and flanks covered.

Horsehunters had dreamed up a wide variety of methods for capturing mustangs. Any or all of them might be useful, depending on the terrain or weather conditions. But the most reliable and most practical way was simply to "walk them down." Two or more men would dog a band of wildlings till they wore down, their resistance softened. A saddle horse's steady, unpanicked gait, even if he was burdened with a rider and gear, could usually outlast the nervous, sporadic pace of the pursued mustangs. The whole job could take four to five patient, tiring days.

In this case they had only to move Soldado's band a short

distance and into the wide, then gradually compressing mouth of the canyon funnel. Even so, it would take time, chousing the animals along so casually that their inevitable fear would climb to a breaking point. . . .

Inside of an hour they were closing in on the mouth of the canyon funnel.

By now the cold had sunk into Parry's marrow; moving his toes and fingers hardly relieved the numbness. He kept a close eye on Tim, who was riding within two hundred feet of him now. The boy seemed all right. Parry's spirits picked up as the canyon rimrock grew into view through the swirling snow.

The next few minutes would tell the story. If Soldado sensed he was being herded into a trap, he would break and so would the others. They might still capture one or two, but the bunch would be lost.

Numb and watchful, the Parrys crowded the animals even closer now. The gray walls of the funnel began to taper inward on either side, and Soldado was clearly getting skittish. The situation presented choices: in front of him the walls were pinching down, but the humans were pushing close behind.

With a snort he trotted deeper into the funnel. The choice was made, the options closed. Parry felt a dry choke of exultance in his throat. *Now!* He drove his mount forward.

"Push 'em, boys! Now—"

The gunshot came flat and hard, as if to shatter his moment of triumph.

Tim's chestnut horse gave a screaming whicker. Parry saw the animal rear up and then go into a frenzied piledriving motion, up and down, his forelegs stiff. Tim cried out once in surprise, then silently fought to keep his seat. The horse was hit; his wild pitchings sent blood spattering across the snow. He was out of his head with pain and panic and Tim had lost all control of him.

Parry opened his mouth to yell at Tim to get off, throw himself clear. But the boy was already losing his seat. Another jolting piledriver spilled him sideways from the saddle. He had the presence of mind to kick his stirrups free and then he smashed into the frozen ground, rolling hard.

Before Parry could rein toward him, another shot came. It screamed off a wind-bared rock less than a yard from Tim. A whole barrage of rifle shots followed, peppering the earth around Tim's prone form, kicking up fans of snow and dirt.

Soldado and his band were already in frenzied motion. Suddenly changing his course, the stallion came veering back the way he'd come. He led his terrified bunch in a thundering stream past Parry and to either side of him, throwing his own mount into panic and momentarily cutting off sight of Tim.

Parry had to fight his spooked horse down with an iron grip, and for a few cursing, careening moments it occupied all his attention. Then Soldado's bunch was past him and gone, and he could see Tim again.

The boy lay sprawled on his side, dazed by the fall, groggily shaking his head. The ground about him was churned to dirty gray furrows by the fusillade of shots, which had suddenly ceased. Tim's face was bleeding.

Get to him!

Parry started to swing off his mount as the rifleman opened up again. He heard the solid *whump* of the bullet and felt a wracking shudder run through his horse. Its knees folded and Parry couldn't scramble away from the falling animal in time. He jerked his left foot free of the stirrup and threw himself sideways, but the horse's dead weight rolled solidly across his lower leg, pinning it from the knee down. Tied to his saddle horn, the packhorse yanked at the line, whickering.

Far on his other side, Linc opened up with his saddle

carbine, directing his fire at the rimrock from which the shots had come. Parry yelled at him to stop; with the enemy laid up in good cover, all he could do was draw fire on himself.

Linc stopped shooting. "Pa," he shouted, "what—"

"Stay where you are!"

Parry cocked his free leg back, braced the foot against the downed animal's saddle at an awkard angle, and shoved with all his strength. His muscles corded and bulged with effort. But neither his pinned leg nor the horse would budge an inch.

Tim was stirring now, pushing to his hands and knees.

"Stay still!" Parry yelled at him.

Frantically, he scanned the rimrock from which the gunfire had come, blinking against the stinging whisks of snow. And couldn't make out a damned thing. He used his teeth to jerk the mitten off his one hand. He tore wildly at the buttons of his Mackinaw, getting it open enough for his hand to claw free the six-gun holstered at his hip and get it out. Still conning the rimrock, he thumbed back the hammer . . . waited.

Ignoring his order, Linc had piled off his horse and was running toward him, carbine in hand. Parry's whole body braced with a sick, reflexive expectancy; he was sure the man on the rim would try to cut Linc down.

But no shot came. In seconds Linc was beside Parry's dead horse, seizing the saddle girth in both hands. He set his heels and strained to lift the horse's weight. "Push, Pa! Help me—" Again Parry thrust against the saddle with his free boot, abetting Linc's tugging. The carcass shifted a little, not enough.

Parry threw an agonized glance at Tim. The boy was floundering dazedly and his boot skidded; he fell on his rear. And again the rifleman began laying down shots all around him.

Christ Jesus!

Parry opened fire at the assailant's spurts of gunflame, pumping off shots as fast as he could. He was shooting half-blind, but maybe he could draw the fellow's fire away from Tim. His hammer fell on a spent shell. The rifleman quit firing at the same time, probably to reload.

Parry's head filled with the pounding roar of his blood as he pushed and Linc pulled in savage, rhythmic heaves. His boot was still wedged under the carcass, but now he was jerking his foot free of the boot, a little at a time.

Suddenly the rifleman resumed firing, his slugs chewing into the earth around Tim. Some glanced in screaming ricochets off patches of flint-frozen soil. He was shooting very close to the boy now, but not, Parry suddenly realized, shooting to hit him, throwing geysers of icy rubble against his body.

Sick with fear for his son, Parry gave a wild, despairing tug at his pinned leg. Suddenly it yanked free. At the same time Tim's shriek cut across the din of rifle fire.

Parry scrambled to his feet and started running toward Tim, who was writhing on the ground. Behind him Linc began shooting at the rimrock as if to cover him. But they were in the open, exposed and helpless. Almost on top of them, yet unseen, a sharpshooter like this one could easily have taken out the three of them stone dead with as many shots.

Why hadn't he?

Parry dropped to the ground by Tim and swooped him into his arms to shield him, putting his own broad back to the rimrock.

But no more shots came. Not even after Linc fired his last round. For a moment they were motionless in position, just listening, Parry on his knees holding the feebly struggling Tim close, Linc standing half-crouched with his carbine held at the ready but useless, hearing nothing now but the low moan of wind.

Slowly, ponderously, Parry stood up, his open mouth gustily frosting his beard. Linc tramped over and peered at Tim. "We better get him out of the wind, Pa."

Parry nodded dumbly. Tim had gone limp in his arms. He carried the boy to a lee of the canyon wall where, between two massive slabs of fallen rimrock, hardly any wind reached. He laid Tim on the ground and said, "Undo his clothes."

Linc opened Tim's coat to reveal a bright welling of blood that soaked his shirtfront. He peeled back the shirt and underwear and they saw where the bullet had gone in.

At first Parry had thought Tim was hit by a chance ricochet. But no ricochet had done this work. A deflected slug would have penetrated at a side-to-upper chest angle. This one had gone in from above, tearing through the left shoulder high on the back and emerging in a mangle of jellied flesh below the left armpit.

Linc said, "I'll get something to tie 'er off. Make compresses, bandages. Couple clean shirts'll do."

He trotted out to his horse standing tranquilly in the wind, its mane and tail furling out. Light snow was already silvering the bay coat of Parry's dead horse. The lead rope fastened to its saddle, the packhorse was trembling and wild-eyed at the close smell of blood. Tim's chestnut had drifted over by the lee, where it stood shuddering but not badly hurt. Blood streaked one haunch and Parry had the dull realization that the rifleman had deliberately shot to crease the animal, send him rearing and plunging.

Linc came back with the shirts. He tore them quickly into uneven strips and folded them into compresses that Parry applied to each side of the wound. In no time they were soaked with blood. Linc ransacked his father's and Tim's saddlebags for more shirts.

Finally they had the bleeding somewhat stanched and had rigged compresses in place with tight bandages that circled Tim's trunk. Then they wrapped him up in three blankets.

In their mutual concern, both Will and Linc had clean forgotten about the rifleman. But he hadn't fired after hitting Tim. Linc suggested that he could get up on the rim by way of a slide that lay up-canyon a piece and have a look-see. Parry promptly vetoed the notion. Aside from the danger, the fellow had probably cleared out. Anyway, they were all sheltered now by the overhang of the rim, safe from any hidden gun.

"Pa, we can't roost here long. Got to be gettin' buckshot to a doctor," Linc said.

Parry nodded wearily, seated on his haunches, cradling Tim in his arms. "Home's a lot nearer than town. I'll take him there on his horse. You make for Salvation the straightest and fastest way you can."

Both of them stood up now, and Linc said quietly, "Someone's going to pay for this work, Pa. Pay hard."

Still gripped by the shock of what had happened and, beyond that, a fear that his thoughts hardly dared touch as yet, Parry felt oddly dazed and detached. Yet his mind fixed with stony clarity on one fact.

Tim had been the bushwhacker's target. Not Linc or Parry himself. All the shooting had been directed at Tim. Or close to him. No shot except maybe that last was intended to kill. Save for the one that had downed Parry's horse. And that was apparently fired to keep him from going to Tim's aid.

But why? God in heaven, why?

CHAPTER FIVE

PARRY RODE INTO HIS RANCH HEADQUARTERS ABOUT MID-afternoon. He was bone-weary and bone-sick, almost numbed through with cold.

He'd had no choice but to ride slowly, resting Tim's blanket-wrapped form on the pommel while he hugged him close, trying to keep him warm. Tim's face was dead white, his lips blue with cold. After a while the numbness and the steady, rocking gait of Tim's chestnut had made Parry's stunned thoughts drift. Sometimes he stopped to check the boy's pulse and rub his flesh and move his limbs a little so that the cold couldn't do its worst. Tim never gave a response except to groan or stir in weak protest. Otherwise Parry gave the chestnut its head and sank into a kind of chilled torpor until he realized that they were crossing the stable pasture and the corrals lay dead ahead. They were home.

Parry shook himself to a wretched alertness and pointed the chestnut toward the house. When he stepped to the ground, his legs nearly caved; his feet were awkward, unfeeling chunks. Lurching onto the porch with Tim, he heard a faint cry from inside, and saw Leah at a window, hand pressed to her mouth. She had the door open as he reached it. . . .

In minutes Leah and Ariel had put Tim to bed. They rubbed him down and washed him and changed his bandage. They bundled him in thick warm blankets and placed heated stones wrapped in gunnysacks at his feet.

Parry slumped in a wooden armchair by the big front parlor fireplace and let the roaring blaze send prickles of fresh sensation through his body. The ruddy warmth peeled back his tiredness and cleared his brain. Tim's horse and the packhorse needed tending. With that thought in mind, he heaved to his feet and tested his legs.

There was a knock at the door and he went to open it. Bill Soholt and Truitt Barrows and Genardo Menocal stood there. Looking out from the bunkhouse, they'd noticed the two horses by the porch and had come to see what was up. Parry told them what had happened and said nothing else could be done till Linc's arrival with Dr. Costiner.

Linc and the doctor rode in fifteen minutes later. Linc had made good time to Salvation, but Doc had been out on a call and Linc could only wait. After Doc's return an hour later, they'd made double time getting here.

Costiner, a pudgy, cherubic, white-bearded sixty-year-old who inevitably put one in mind of St. Nicholas, was with Tim for an hour. Then he came out and gave them a bushel of anatomical information, the gist of which was that the left scapula ("That's the shoulder blade") and two ribs were broken but that no vital organ had been seriously damaged. It was still a damned serious wound. He told them to expect fever and chills, and explained when and how to administer the medicines he was leaving with them: laudanum for pain, quinine for fever. He thought Tim had a good chance, better than touch-and-go, but he was going to be a mighty sick lad for a long time. If his condition took a serious turn for the worse, Costiner was to be summoned at once.

After the doctor left, there were the usual workaday things to be done, things a body did almost by habit. Only now they went about them under a numbing freight of worry. Ariel took up the watch in Tim's room. Leah began to prepare supper. Parry and Linc and the three hands went about the before-supper chores.

Working alongside Bill Soholt and Truitt as they grained and watered the horses, Parry felt more of the numbness leave him. His brain had absorbed what had happened and a hot wrath was starting to scour through him like white flame. Now he could talk fully about what had happened. And did.

"If it was Virg," Soholt said soberly, "he takes some damned hard learning."

"Lemme tell you something," Truitt said. "I don't reckon Virg had aught to do with it. Oh shit, yeah, he's a hardnosed ol' boy. I can see Virg doing what whoever done t'other night with the windows and chickens, if he was het up enough and had a little snake-eye in him. That's one thing. But Jesus, Mr. Parry. What happened to Timmy . . . that's a whole different ball o' wax."

Soholt nodded, glancing at Parry. "For once I'd say Truitt's head's holding something solider'n hair and a hat. I read Virg that way, too."

Slowly Parry shook his head. "I'm just not sure. He gave me vow he was going to nail my balls to an outback. How far would he go?"

"Might bear you a personal grudge and sit on it a long time," Soholt said. "But taking it out on your boy . . . it don't fit Virg's style somehow."

Maybe not, Parry thought bleakly. Whether it did or didn't, he was a target in a deadlier way than he could have dreamed. And so, he could now be sure, was his family. Whoever had shot his son had really been aiming, in an oblique, dead-cold way, at *him*. Parry felt the conviction in his guts, like ice.

Soholt said, "Will, it comes back to what we said t'other night. There's a pure crazy out to you."

"Even a crazy man has got to have a reason."

"Not one as makes any sense to us, maybe. Not if he's loonie enough."

Fine. Where did that leave all of them? Like sitting ducks—no matter who the enemy was. Dr. Costiner had said he'd tell Alder Kane about the shooting, and Parry meant to ride in tomorrow and talk it over with Kane himself.

For all the damned good it'll do!

At supper, Parry repeated his previous order that everybody was to stick close to the place, to keep guns at hand, to stay on their guard. Not that the warning was necessary, but he wanted to stress it. They took his words in silence, eating without real appetite. Bill and Truitt and Genardo finished up quickly, muttered their good nights and left for the bunkhouse.

Linc went upstairs to relieve Ariel, who came down to supper. She entered the kitchen and took her place silently, eyes downcast. She took small helpings of everything and then picked at them. Both she and her mother had done a little crying. No hysteria. They weren't the kind. Both were red-eyed and sniffling just a bit. It was all right for a woman to give vent to her feelings. A man wasn't supposed to. What a man usually did was put down a few stiff drinks.

Maybe later, Parry could afford to. And even invite Linc (who'd taken just one sip of booze in his young life and then spat it out in disgust) to join him. If Linc didn't want to, that was all right.

Parry packed his pipe, struck a match and drew the pipe alight, looking at his daughter across the matchflame. Ariel's fingers were raw, a little swollen, inflamed by a rash of tiny cuts.

Up through yesterday, she'd worked steadily at cleaning up the mess left by the shot-out windows. Broken glass had littered every room in the house. All of it had to be swept up. All carpets and rag rugs had to be carried outside, hung on a clothesline, and beaten free of glass particles. All the shards of glass remaining in the window frames had to be pried out and squares of oiled paper fastened over the holes. (Clevenger's General Merchandise Store in Salvation hadn't been able to fill Parry's big order for glass, so it would have to be shipped from Cheyenne.) Finally, the whole house had to be swept once more, room by room, to catch any residual debris of splinters. There hadn't been too much breakage aside from the windows. Ariel had lost a china cat she'd treasured. A couple of wall-mounted lithographs and a big oil painting of her maternal grandfather (that grim old man she'd never met) had suffered damage. She'd valued those, too. But never a word of complaint out of Ariel.

A fine girl, for all her streak of mischief that sometimes worried him. A fine daughter. Best a man could ask for. Even if she did tend to flirt a bit with the likes of Truitt Barrows.

Still, what could you expect? Living way out in the backwoods, with no close neighbors, Truitt being the only young man around (even if he was a little old for her). Understandable, in a girl approaching womanhood.

And, Parry realized with a mildly guilty shock, Ariel was about to turn the ripe age of sixteen. Turning point in a girl's life, some claimed. Like a lot of men (maybe most), he had a hell of a time remembering birthdays, anniversaries, and the like. If Leah didn't remind him, he'd almost invariably forget they were coming up.

"Sis," he said gently.

Ariel quit stirring the food around on her plate and looked up at him.

"Happy birthday," Parry said. "You'll be having one in, what is it, about three days—"

"Two, Daddy."

"Sure. Sorry I didn't think of it. Could have bought you a gift, some little thing, when I was in town last."

"That's all right." Ariel managed a smile. "I guess it's about the last thing you'd have on your mind right now."

"Reckon we can make it up to you later."

Leah had returned to the table after clearing away some of the dishes. She laid a hand on Ariel's shoulder and smiled at Parry. "Of course we will. This isn't the time to worry about it."

Unbidden, he felt a mighty surge of love for both of them.

A man placed a sight of store in his sons. They were a prefiguring, in a way, of the immortality he might never be sure of knowing except through them. A girl child of his flesh and blood was different. She was the fragile incarnation of womanhood; the wife he loved born again. Born to be cherished and protected at all costs. Maybe that was where a man's feelings lay most open, where he was most vulnerable. God, if anything ever happened to either of them, Leah or Ariel . . .

Abruptly, Parry got up, walked over to the big Monarch stove, and lifted a front lid. He knocked the dottle of his pipe into the glowing coals and gruffly said he was going to have a look outside. He went to the door, opened it, and stepped out on to the back porch.

It was full dark and the stars made frosty points against a cobalt sky. The wind and blowing snow had died off earlier. Everything was sugared with a dusting of snow, white as milk under the starlight. He could pick out details clear as day. The night was dead silent. The windows of the bunkhouse burned yellow warm in the whiteness. A tree bough snapped with cold. Stillness again.

Danger? If any lurked out there, how did a man go about second-guessing it?

Parry stepped back inside, then went upstairs to check on Tim, who was stirring fitfully in his sleep, feverish. Linc looked tuckered out, but insisted he was good for a couple hours watch. Tired or not, he added, he didn't think any of them would sleep too soundly tonight.

"Pa, it looks like that so-and-so has his sights on all of us. One at a time."

"Maybe. But I'm the target, Linc."

Linc nodded. "Getting at you through us."

"That's my feeling."

"If it's Virg, you got the why-for."

Parry nodded tiredly, baffled. He didn't think Linc believed it either.

Going downstairs, he dug out his account books and spread them on the kitchen table. The accounts were balanced to date, nothing to be gained by checking the figures again. It was a diversion, that was all. The cool logic of mathematics against the icy illogic of a nightmare that was crossing into reality. . . .

Barney raised his head and growled.

Ordinarily they ignored the big hound's occasional rumblings. He was apt to growl or bark at any odd sound or imagined menace that tickled his fancy. Now, edgy as they all were, they stopped what they were doing and looked at him.

Leah was washing the dishes, Ariel was drying them. Barney was stretched under the table, crowded against Parry's feet. Now he got up, paced across the floor and back, then stopped and looked at the door.

Ariel said, "Looks like he has to go. Should I let him out?"

"Wait," Parry said.

Barney's head sank between his shoulders. The fur bristled along his spine. His lips peeled off his fangs in a deeply guttural snarl. Then he began barking frantically. Parry came to his feet and started for the door.

"Will!" Leah said softly and urgently. "Don't go out. Don't show yourself—"

He'd intended to open the door only a crack, enough to see out. But as Leah spoke, a bullet plowed through the thick layer of oiled paper across one of the kitchen windows, tearing it half away. The slug crashed into a pile of utensils beside the sink.

Ariel screamed. A second shot hammered into the wall next to Leah. It knocked out a chunk of plaster six inches from her shoulder and she cried out as well.

"Down!" Parry bellowed.

He dived for the door, grabbed up his gun from the table beside it, and plunged outside. A glance backward showed him Leah and Ariel sinking down on their heels, Leah gripping the wildly yapping Barney by his collar to hold him back. Parry banged the door shut.

A third shot split the night and he heard it *snap* in the cold air and then bury itself in the doorjamb inches away. He saw gunflame, too, and brought his pistol up as a form detached itself from the squared, dark shape of the woodshed, angling away at a bent-over run toward a nearby pile of logs.

Parry got the running figure in his sights, led it a little, and fired. The shot went low, kicking up a floury fan of snow. The man reached the log pile and fired from its shelter. His slug screamed off the big grindstone a few yards from the porch, a wild shot.

The bunkhouse door was flung open, two men spilling out past the lamplight. Soholt and then Truitt, and both had rifles. The attacker broke away from the woodpile, in full retreat now. He was heading wide of the corrals, making a straight run toward the fir grove. He was a clear target against snow and starlight. Parry fired. The man kept running. Moments later Soholt and Truitt fired at the same time. Parry thought the figure jerked and broke stride. But he kept going, vanishing among the trees.

Parry pounded across the yard, pulling up beside Bill and Truitt.

Soholt said, "Now he's in cover and we got to go in after him. If you want him."

"Get our asses shot off, could be," Truitt said. "But I'm game."

Parry nodded. It would be a risky business, but there were three of them . . . four, he silently amended, for Linc had come out of the house and was running this way, rifle in hand.

"If we let him make it away, he'll just be back," Parry said.

"That's right," Truitt said. "He likely got a horse hid back in the trees."

As Linc joined them, Parry said, "We'll split up and come in on the trees from two sides. Try to catch him between us. But be careful, damn it. You can't make out much but a man's outline. Don't get shooting at each other."

"He got a hat on," Soholt observed. "None of us has. That'll show him up clear."

"All right, but take care."

They split apart and started around the corrals, Soholt and Truitt to the left, Parry to the right with Linc pacing, at his father's order, close behind rather than at his side.

Coming around back of the corrals, they loped quickly across a brief open space and slipped into the trees. There was a muffled cracking of brush, a man's hoarse yell from somewhere in the grove. Then a louder sound of splintering boughs as a heavy body burst through the trees.

It was very close, just a few yards to their right, and they had their rifles up as the horse came racing out of the grove. Free of the trees, it broke into a run. But it was riderless.

"My guess," whispered Linc, "is he come up next his

horse and tried getting on. But he smelled of blood. Spooked it.''

Parry didn't reply. They had his location fixed where the yell had sounded. Parry led the way, sliding almost noiselessly between the snow-crusted branches. The man's tracks showed faintly on the floor of the grove where snow lay white and sparkling, the fir trunks black against it. Coatless, Parry felt the cold bite through his thick wool shirt.

Suddenly a shot came. Then another.

Parry increased his pace, slamming ahead through the branches, powder snow dusting his face. He heard the sharp lift of Soholt's and Truitt's voices, and now Soholt called "Will?" and he answered.

The four of them converged on the small clearing at the same time. The snow was trampled and darkness stained a patch of it. Soholt struck a match and held it hand-cupped. A great splash of blood made a raggedly steaming hole in the snow and straggled off to the side.

The man had fallen here. He'd made it back to his feet and staggered off into the trees.

"Hit bad," Soholt said. "He ain't going far."

They followed the floundering trail of tracks and blood drops through the grove to its north end. Here, at the edge of trees, the man had fallen sidelong in the snow. His eyes were closed and he looked as peaceful as if he'd gone to sleep.

Soholt knelt down and struck a match, holding it close to the dead face of Virg Bollinger.

"Goddlemighty and Satan's socks," Truitt Barrows said. "It's him right enough. But I wouldn't a believed it. No sir, I wouldn't."

CHAPTER SIX

NEXT DAY THE WEATHER TOOK ANOTHER SUDDEN TURN. THE belated blast of winter faded under a warm sun and a thaw wind. By late afternoon, the light crust of snow had almost vanished. Tim's fever peaked with an amazing quickness and then broke, and he fell into a fitful sleep. By nightfall everyone was pretty well over their jitters and the Parry household was somewhat back to normal, at least in an outward way.

By now, though, Will Parry had another concern on his mind. Doc Costiner had said he would notify the sheriff of what had happened to Tim. Knowing Alder Kane, you'd expect him to be out at WP headquarters the next morning, to ask his questions and get an investigation under way. When Kane hadn't shown up by evening, Parry decided he'd go to town the next morning and find out what was up. And he could take in Virg Bollinger's body for a coroner's inquest.

By breakfast time, Tim was sluggishly awake. After Leah and Ariel had changed his bandages, he was able to take a few swallows of beef broth. Today was Ariel's sixteenth birthday, but she seemed more downcast than set up about it. Parry tried to cheer her up, saying that this time he'd be sure and remember to bring her a gift from town.

"That's all right, Daddy," she said with a wan smile. "You don't have to."

Parry gave the crew their orders for the day and then tramped out of the house, thinking, *Women!* All the real trouble was past, but maybe Ariel was in a condition of monthly "blues" or something. Uneasily, he backed his thoughts away from the matter. With a girl, best to let her mother handle that sort of thing.

He hitched the team to the spring wagon and drove over to the tackshed where they'd taken Virg Bollinger's body. He loaded Virg's stiffened, canvas-wrapped corpse into the wagon bed, climbed back to the seat, hoorawed the team into motion, and headed west toward Salvation.

The morning was pleasant enough, the driving easy, and the light snowmelt had made only a mild mire of the road ruts. Idly picking at his own rather glum mood, Parry thought he ought to feel better than he did. Tim was already on the mend; the menace that had stalked the family was put down.

What seemed contrariwise about the situation, ran his old lawman's instinct, was a jogging out of pattern. Virg's attack two nights ago hadn't been worthy of his previous efforts. Almost clumsy, compared to what he had done before. But did it really mean anything, this lingering uneasiness Parry felt? Nerves, he told himself. You're bound to have a bad case . . . after all that. It was Virg. No doubt about it now.

Riding into Salvation by late morning, Parry stopped at Nils Nansen's smithy and learned the reason that Alder Kane hadn't dropped out yesterday.

"Down sick," Nils said, peering into the wagon bed. "But Doc told him about Virg. You done up Virg all good and neat for the coroner, *ja*?"

"Yes. What's the matter with Al? Is it bad?"

"Bad enough to lay him up awhile, whatever. Alder, he claims it was an attack of indigestion. Doc Costiner thinks maybe it's his heart. The missus and me, we drop over to

see Al last night. He is sitting up, looking pretty good.
But . . ." Nils lifted and settled a massive shoulder. "Man
his age, who knows for sure?"

"Did Doc listen to his heart?"

"*Ja*. Said there ain't no dis . . . uh, disrhythm he can
tell. But them dumb wood stethoscopes, I never see how
any sawbones can tell nothing with one of them. I bet you,
by *Gud*, a man could invent a better one."

Parry grinned. "There's your next undertaking, then."

"Maybe. Ain't nothing in wood a man can't do better in
iron." Nils brightened a little. "Say, that contraption I am
fixing for you, it's coming along good, Will. Soon as I work
out a few more ideas on it, be ready for you to wear. Be
good as a brand new arm, by *Gud*!"

Parry said agreeably, "Well, here's hoping," and didn't
feel a trace of hope that it would be. "I have a few things to
take care of, Nils. You're not too busy, we can go for a beer
later on."

"Sure. I show you what I got done on the contraption
then, too."

Parry left Virg Bollinger's corpse at the undertaking
parlor of Jase Metcalf, who was also the county coroner.
Afterward he drove on to Clevenger's General Merchandise
Store, left the team and wagon at the hitchrail, and went
inside to buy a few items that Leah wanted, also to see if he
could find a likely birthday present.

Remembering Ariel's prized china cat that had been a
casualty to gunfire, he wondered if he could replace it.
Clevenger had no cats in stock, but he showed Will a
matched pair of three-inch-high china bulldogs, a sample of
the notions he kept on hand for the ladies' trade, and Parry
bought them on the spot. Clevenger, who also served as the
U.S. postmaster, brought out an accumulation of mail for
the Parrys that had arrived a day ago. There were two letters
from Will's father, one from a maiden aunt of his, and

(amazingly) one letter apiece from Leah's father and her mother who, unforgiving of her decision to marry the son of a stable groom, rarely unbent enough to keep in touch with her. And there was a hefty pile of magazines and newspapers to which the Parrys were at pains to subscribe, so they and the kids wouldn't be isolated altogether from the outside world. Done up in bundles were copies of *The Atlantic Monthly, Harper's Weekly, Godey's Lady's Book* (for Ariel's training), the *New York Daily Herald*, the *Boston Globe-Chronicle*, and even *The Times* of London.

After depositing his few purchases and letters and many packages of periodicals under the seat of his wagon, Parry set off down a side street toward Alder Kane's home.

It was a big, double-storied frame affair that until recently had housed quite a brood of children. Kane had married rather late in life, but the last of his grown kids had finally gone out on their own, and now the sheriff and his middle-aged wife, Kate, lived alone.

Kate, buxom and red-haired Irish and briskly no nonsense, answered Parry's knock. She looked a little harried. "Come in, Will. Glad to see you. Maybe *you* can be talking some sense into the old fool!"

"What's the trouble?" Parry asked as he took off his hat and entered the front parlor. "I heard about Al's indigestion . . . or whatever—"

"It's more'n likely his heart and Costiner ordered him to rest for a week. Now himself wants to be getting right out and back on the job and I'm telling him *no!*"

"Damn it, don't talk about me like I'm not here!" Alder Kane, who hardly ever lifted his voice, half-shouted from the next room. "That you, Will?"

Parry followed Kate into the back parlor, where Kane was sitting in a leather upholstered armchair, fully dressed.

"Sit down, Will," he said testily. "And don't try to talk

me out of anything. Man's got a job and it's his to do, nobody else's, he's got to by God be about it."

Kate had a jaw like a sprung trap and she thrust it out. "He does *not*! Don't be blathering any more about 'a touch of indigestion,' either!"

Parry sat down on a straight-backed chair and said, "What's so urgent, Al? Doc's told you about Virg, that's done with. It's all the excitement there's been hereabouts in a coon's age."

"There's another thing, now." Kane was perspiring a little and his color was high. It wasn't healthy color, Parry thought. Sort of pink and frazzled, sallow around the edges. "At Horrid Hattie's fancy house, you know, down by the river?"

"Well—" Parry cleared his throat. "Not by personal acquaintance."

"Anyway," Kane went on, "one of Hattie's girls has turned up missing. Seems this wh—this girl, Maybelle, stepped outside for a breath of air last night between tr— well, she stepped outside and never came back. Benjy, that old colored man who does chores for Hattie, took a look around first light this morning. Found signs of a scuffle right outside. 'Peared to him that the girl was carried off. Just a kid she was, sixteen she claimed, but Benjy doubts she was even that. He brought me the word this morning."

Parry had been hunched forward, elbows on his knees, dangling his hat in his hands. Now he straightened in the chair, feeling a prickle of gooseflesh at the back of his neck.

"That's all he found? No tracks going away?"

"Benjy said not. None he could pick up, leastways, and he scouted some for the army in his younger days. Seems the girl was just packed up and carried off somewhere. Must of been a strong son that done it. Not much of a scuffle, Benjy said, and none that anyone heard."

"Did he look out and around the place a ways?"

"He did. Turned up no other sign. Nothing." Kane's tendoned hands gripped the chair arms. "God . . . takes a special kind of ba—rotten stripe of man to carry off a child, even if she was . . ."

"You can be saying 'tricks' and 'whore' and 'bastard' plain out, Mr. Kane," Kate said with a touch of acid satisfaction. "You'd say the words if you was talking to either of us alone. Will Parry's not a shy man and it wasn't in any convent I was raised."

"That you surely weren't, mavournin," Kane said, fervently and only a little wryly. "But, Will, I . . ."

"You'll do what your wife and your doctor say," Parry told him. "I did a little lawdogging in my time, remember? I can do a little right now. Fill in for you."

"Will, there's no need—"

"Reckon there's a need, all right, and folks around here pull together when there is." Parry rose to his feet. "I can go ask some questions. Over at Hattie's and around that neighborhood. Maybe somebody saw something, heard something. You never know."

Alder Kane objected again, but not so strenuously, and he slumped back in his chair. He made only a token response to Kate's vehement backing of Parry's offer. Parry barely listened to their words.

Something about this business sent a ghostly and uneasy thread of memory tingling along his nerves. He brushed the feeling away, along with the train of thought it tended to stir up. Don't start to spook yourself, he thought. You don't know anything.

Then he remembered that he'd thought the same thing when all the trouble just past had started up.

Alder Kane reluctantly agreed to let Parry do some spadework, at least. Ask around and see if anybody had even a suggestive hint of what had happened to the girl Maybelle.

Sick or not, Kane was a thorough man. He wanted to hear Parry's own account of the events that began with Tim's wounding and culminated in the death of Virg Bollinger. Parry told him everything in detail, and he sensed that Alder Kane, too, wasn't quite easy in his mind about the whole matter. Any man involved in law work gained a sixth sense about such things, even when there was nothing he could quite put his finger on.

Talking it over, though, they agreed that there was nothing to go on outside of what they knew for sure. All a man could do was keep on the alert for a reasonable spell, see if anything else came up, and try to head off whatever looked suspicious.

Still, Parry began silently to wish that he'd renewed a warning to his family and the crew before he'd left headquarters this morning. To stay on the lookout. Stick close to the place. Then, it had seemed unnecessary. Now, he felt a little less sure.

Kane removed the worn, shiny sheriff's star from his vest and handed it to Parry. "Son, that's my badge of authority. You show it to anyone doesn't feel like talking right up. You ask your questions, get your answers, and bring 'em back to me."

Parry said his good-byes to the Kanes and headed back for the crooked straggle of Salvation's main street.

More and more, he felt like a man sparring with shadows. The phlegmatic side of his nature told him: *Don't be an unaccountable damn fool. It will only take a little while to do this job for Al. Damn it, you've had odd feelings about things before and mostly they never came to anything. Everyone has 'em.*

At Main Street, Parry made a right turn and swung west toward where it branched off onto River Street. Lined almost exclusively with saloons and brothels, River Street lay just south of the railroad tracks, a kind of magical dividing line in almost any community, here or back East. The respectable folk stayed north of the tracks and pretended—at least the ladies did—that "across the tracks" hardly existed.

Once you stepped onto River Street, you could spot at once Horrid Hattie's establishment, with the huge black-letter sign printed across its white-clapboarded front: HARRIET'S BOARDING ACADEMY. Houses of ill repute usually identified themselves by such euphemisms, but other local madams had put out signs that were discreetly small and unobtrusive. Only Harriet, or Hattie, seemed to flaunt a defiant pride in her trade.

As Parry came abreast of the railroad depot and was about to cross the tracks, Earl Miner, the slight and bespectacled station agent, stepped out on the depot platform and hailed him.

"Will, hey!" Earl was waving a piece of yellow paper in his hand. "This just came in over the wire for you."

The railroad depot was also the telegraph office, but Parry had never received a telegram in all his sixteen years in this Wyoming basin. He halted in surprise for a moment, then veered over to the platform.

Earl handed him the paper, saying, "Just good luck you're in town, Will. Was about to send a boy out to your place with this. Don't know what it's all about, but looks to be what my Texas kinfolk used to call a ringtail wowser."

Parry stared at the yellow paper, feeling his guts turn to ice.

Earl had simply jotted down the message in his broad, sprawling hand. But he was a good speller and the words were legible enough . . . and chillingly clear.

Trinidad Colo. To William Parry Salvation Wyo. Josey Mast escaped from Joliet 6 wks ago. Remember what he said at his trial. Now Judge J T Venner is dead.

Also Sgt Sean Mulhare. Both killed by unknown assailants. Just learned about all this. Keep a good watch and do not repeat do not try to make any move on your own. Will be at your ranch as soon as I can get there. Tom Redfern.

Sweet Jesus.

Parry let the paper fall from his hand. His thoughts went out of focus. For a moment he stared straight ahead of him and didn't see anything.

"Hey? Will?"

Parry's attention pulled back to Earl Miner's face.

"My God," said Earl. "Man, you look like you just saw a ghost. All that bad?"

Parry didn't reply. No room in his thoughts for answers. He looked blankly at Earl for another moment, then pivoted on his heel and headed back upstreet at a pounding run. He had no thought for anything but to get back to WP headquarters and his family.

His family. Unwarned and unaware and unprotected . . .

CHAPTER SEVEN

Ariel Parry was bitterly bored.

For two days she'd had the task of staying in her room so she could check occasionally on her brother Tim and be in easy earshot if he should wake up and want anything. But mostly he just slept, fitfully rousing from time to time. Mildly dosed with opiates that Dr. Costiner had left, he was too dull and drowsy even to exchange insults with her, and Ariel was sick of waiting on him. With squares of oiled paper nailed over the window, only a low-turned lamp relieved the gloom of her little chamber. It did nothing to heighten her spirits.

This morning she'd halfheartedly tried to reread three novels expressly forbidden to her—Zola's *La Confession de Claude*, *Thérèse Raquin*, and *L'Assommoir*—that a reprobate uncle, her mother's brother, had sent her a couple years ago. Will and Leah had decreed them unfit for a young girl, but retained them for their own library, which Ariel considered downright unjust. Inevitably, she'd sneak the books to her own room once in awhile and peruse them. Avidly, at first. Later on wondering what was so terrible about them. They sure were a loss as to entertainment. All she got out of going through them was a mild relish in defying parental interdict. And by now the books seemed pretty stale.

Ariel tried to get up a stir of excitement wondering what

Daddy might fetch her from town. He was quite good about observing birthdays and the like, getting small presents for each of them—as long as Ma reminded him that a special day was coming up. But wondering didn't slake her boredom for very long.

What a way to spend her sixteenth birthday!

Feeling rebellious now, she slid off her bed, went to the window, and carefully tugged a corner of oiled paper free of the lower sash, trying not to tear it too much. She put her face to the triangle of sunlight.

Oh Lordy, it was a beautiful day. Out beyond the buildings, the meadow flats that her father called the stable pasture—because his horses ranged there in season—rolled away like a greening carpet. The sun poked warmly at her face; a wildflower breeze blew through the gap and tickled her restless spirits even more.

Lordy. I just have to get outside for a spell or I will go absolutely crazy.

Ariel gave a determined hitch to her shoulders, gathered up the Zola novels, and returned them to a shelf in her parents' room. After looking in on Tim and finding him sound asleep, she marched downstairs to the kitchen. Leah, sleeves rolled to the elbows and hands covered with flour, was punching up a batch of bread dough.

She gave her daughter a fleeting smile. "Everything all right, dear?"

"Sure. Tim is really sawing wood up there. His color is fine." Ariel folded her arms and leaned her shoulder against the doorjamb. "Ma, would it be okay if I went outside awhile?"

"Of course. You can't just sit around for so long. Go outside, walk about and limber up a bit."

It wasn't quite what Ariel had in mind. She said swiftly, "What I mean, Ma, would it be all right if I hitch up the old buckboard and take a little drive?"

"No," Leah said flatly.

"Ma," Ariel went on stubbornly, "suppose that I ask Truitt to hitch up and I go for a drive with him. He can handle the horses and all that. I could just sit on the seat and be quiet. Wouldn't *that* be all right?"

Leah stopped kneading the bread. "Careful, young lady. That comes mighty close to being sass."

"I'm sorry. But really, on my birthday and all . . . I'm *sixteen* now. And it's not like Truitt was my *beau* or anything."

"I should hope not." Leah hesitated. "I suppose . . . there'd be no harm in it. I can look in on Timmy, meantime. But mind you, I'll expect you back in an hour. And you are not to go any great distance."

The concession surprised Ariel; she hadn't really expected it. Linc and Bill Soholt were out scouring the draws to see what kind of winterkill their cattle might have suffered, and old Genardo was too arthritic to handle the reins of a team. That left only Truitt Barrows to take her for a drive. All the same, knowing that both Will and Leah considered Truitt to be an unsuitable sort, except in casual company, she was surprised.

"Thanks, Ma!"

She started to leave the kitchen before her mother had second thoughts. Leah said sharply, "Just a moment. Are you wearing your corset? You're not, are you?"

Ariel sighed. "No'm."

"You are certainly not going for a ride in the company of a young man without wearing a proper corset. Put it on. And a bonnet, too."

Resignedly, Ariel trudged upstairs, took off her dress, and wrestled into the rib-gripping garment of whalebone stays and reinforced stitching that she'd been ordered to start wearing a month ago. Another introduction to womanhood that she already loathed. It felt like being encased in armor. Over it she donned a fresh, crisp frock, tied a matching calash over her red hair, pinched her cheeks for color, then left the house and hurried down to the corral.

Truitt and Genardo Menocal were preparing to work over a green mustang.

They'd driven the refractory animal into a narrow handling chute between the small holding pen and the big breaking corral. Truitt was red-faced and swearing a blue streak as he worked at putting a double-rigged saddle and braided hackamore on the shuffling, snorting mustang. Ariel pressed up to the corral poles and folded her arms chin-high on one, watching.

At last Truitt succeeded in getting the saddle and hackamore rigged in place. He swung to the top of the chute and lowered himself into the saddle. "Let 'er rip," he told Genardo, and the old man swung open the gate.

The paint mustang came high-rolling into the corral, plunging up and down in great jolting leaps that it seemed should wrench a man's spine apart. Quite suddenly he switched to sunfishing, forcing Truitt to continually shift his body for balance. He took it in easy stride, doffing his hat and waving it, side-slipping toothy grins at Ariel as he showed off. Then, as the mustang began to "pioneer," changing directions at every leap, Truitt quit clowning and concentrated on holding his seat.

A man's frame couldn't absorb such punishment for long, and Ariel thought that Genardo let it go on for a dangerously long time before he ordered Truitt to take a dive. He hit the corral dust in a horsebreaker's loose roll, scrambling away from the driving hoofs and out through the corral poles.

"*Bueno*, heh, heh," Genardo said with satisfaction. "We make a *jinete* of you yet, you don' get busted to flinders first. Heh, heh. *Bueno*."

Truitt said, "The hell with you," and grinned whitely at Ariel as he climbed to his feet, limping a little. "Hey there,

Longlaigs! You come to watch me bust the vinegar out o' this sandy one?"

Ariel half lidded her eyes in what she fancied was a sultry way. "You better be careful," she said. "If my dad heard you call me that, would he give you the what-for."

Truitt whooped. "Oh sure. He just mop up the cowshed floor with me, I bet."

Ariel gave him a radiant smile. "Well, you remember what happened to Virg Bollinger when he whipped that horse. If you can remember that far back."

"You pretty full of sap and sass, missy. Think you're so blamed smart."

"Would you like to take me for a drive, Truitt?"

Truitt blinked. His jaw dropped. "Honest Injun?"

"No you don'," Genardo said wickedly. "You don' quit work till I say you quit. I say you top that *caballo* again, *muchacho*."

"Oh, but, Genardo," Ariel murmured. "Ma said Truitt is supposed to take me for a drive. And she has the say-so when Daddy is away. Hasn't she?"

"Goddom," old Genardo fumed. "Is no time to stop the work. This *caballo*, I wan' to get him broke right away."

"Just ain't your day, *viejo*," Truitt said delightedly. "Reckon I can hitch up that ol' buckboard of your daddy's, Longl—Miss Ariel. Kinda bunged-up old buggy, but I reckon it'll hold together. . . ."

Truitt was all courtesy now. He gave her a proper hand up to the buckboard seat, climbed up beside her, and expertly took up the reins. "You got a hankering which way you want to go, Miss Ariel?"

"Oh, across the stable pasture, I guess. If it's not too rough for this rickety old rig."

"Ain't this a hummer, though!" Truitt said happily, and got the team moving.

As soon as they were a ways from the house, cut off from

sight of it by a thick arm of fir trees, Ariel took off her bonnet and let the breeze blow through her hair. She thought with pleasure of how scandalized Ma would be if she knew. She liked Truitt's appreciative gaze.

"Boy, is this a hummer," he said.

Ariel batted her eyes and smiled into his happy ruddy face. Didn't he fancy himself the high, wide, and handsome one! What a big dumb thing he was. But feeling him close beside her, burly-shouldered and slim-hipped, long and catty with lean muscle, she felt a mild simmer of excitement. Sweat patched his dusty clothes and a good fresh man-and-horse smell lifted off him. It was fun to tease Truitt a little, so long as she didn't carry it too far. He was too old for her to fool with. Lordy, he must be twenty-one or so.

"Say," Truitt said seriously, "maybe you could tell me something I am right curious about."

"What is that?"

"Ariel, that's a funny kind o' handle. Where you get that from?"

"Oh, I guess Daddy and Ma thought it would be a likely name for a girl. Ariel was a sprite. In *The Tempest*."

"Uh . . . ?"

"A sprite is a kind of elf or fairy. *The Tempest* is a play by William Shakespeare."

Truitt's face brightened. "Oh, sure. I hear tell 'bout him. He took a heap of good sayings folks made up—you hear 'em all the time. You know, like 'handsome is as handsome does'? And he put all them sayings in those plays of his. That's what I heard tell."

Ariel opened her mouth and then closed it. Finally she said, "I never thought of that. I guess that's what he did."

At the end of the stable pasture, the land climbed into the long east slopes of the valley. An old Indian trail, worn at least a foot below the level of the surrounding ground by generations of tribal migration, curved through the Buck-horn Hills.

Truitt had a sure hand with the team, guiding them along the broad, uneven trail. It led among sparse, wind-twisted pines and patches of scrub oak growing out of shallow soil that overlay eroded crags, the remnants of which split out of the ground like stone fangs. In other places they reared up in miniature hanging cliffs, broken and rough, that sheltered dells where larkspur and strawberry plants and mushrooms poked up through loam and pine needles. Going east, the hills and cliffs would become steeper, dropping off at last to the roiling current of the Buckhorn River where it coiled and crawled out of the mountains, forming the east boundary of the WP ranch.

In less than a half mile, though, Ariel decided they had gone far enough.

"I guess you can turn back now, Truitt."

He pulled up the team with a word and a light hand to the reins, then gazed at her disappointedly. "That wa'n't much of a drive."

"It wasn't, was it? But I'll catch aitch-ee-double-ell from Ma if I don't get back inside the hour. We'll be running a little over it, at that."

Mischief glinted in Truitt's eyes. "Well, you couldn't catch much worse aitch, then. Can't we jus'—"

"No," Ariel said demurely but firmly. "You know Daddy and Ma are still pretty much set up after all that's happened. And I have an injured brother to look after. You don't want to catch aitch too, do you? Gee, Truitt. You might even get fired."

Grumbling, Truitt swung the wagon around, crowding offside on the trail as he did so. Suddenly Ariel gripped his arm, then quickly dropped her hand.

Truitt pulled the team up at once. "What's 'at for?"

"Never mind," Ariel said between her teeth. "Just drive us home, will you?"

Something in her tone made Truitt put the team ahead without question.

Ariel had seen the man just as the wagon swung around.

On a rise less than a hundred yards to the left of them was a stand of scrub oak, its branches still winter-bare. The trees were close together, but the shape of a horse and rider showed plain among them, dark among the dark tree trunks.

A man just sitting on his horse. That alone was enough to send a dark chill through Ariel.

A man mysteriously sitting his horse among the trees. Doing nothing else. Just watching them, apparently. Some hill man, more than likely. A lone trapper, white or Indian. Or a stranger to the country, a grubline drifter. That was all.

And yet . . .

"Would you hurry up, please?" Ariel said nervously.

Truitt scowled. "Say, what is't? You—"

"Just move the horses along, will you!"

Truitt muttered something and shook the team into a faster pace, urging them almost to a perilous clip along the hairpin twists of the old trail to show his irritation.

"Don't, for heaven's sake!" Ariel cried. "Do you want to turn us over?"

"You said—"

"I know what I said. Now slow down a little!"

She gripped the edge of the seat tightly in her hands, not daring to look back. Ahead of them, she saw with small relief, the rugged upper trail was breaking away into the level ground of the lower flats.

Against the nameless terror threading her veins, Ariel threw a glance back across her shoulder.

He was there. Seen in fleeting glimpses among the barelimbed trees that crowded the tight turns of the trail, he was following them at a measured distance. Holding his horse to a steady lope a couple hundred feet or so to their rear.

"Oh God," Ariel whispered. "Truitt, hurry up!"

"You jus' said—"

"There's someone following us!"

"Huh—?" Truitt cast a bewildered glance backward. "Goddlemighty and Satan's socks. He is, ain't he? Say, this is mighty peculiar, now. I wonder who—"

"Never mind who! He's up to no good. I know it! Truitt, will you *get moving*?"

Truitt's brow was knit in puzzlement, but he felt the force of her terror. Not hesitating now, he savagely gigged the team onward, careening dangerously around the last sharp turns.

The trail ahead rolled straight off the slope where it gentled away into the flats. Now Truitt could safely put the team into an all-out run. He gave the reins a lashing motion, hoorawing the horses at the top of his voice.

The trail leveled out now, lumpy but on an even course west toward the stable pasture. Ariel gritted her teeth and winced each time the wheels hit a bump. A little more punishment would break this old rig apart. The wind mussed her hair, blowing it around her face. The bonnet she'd laid in her lap blew away, tumbling off behind the wagon, and she barely noticed it.

She gripped the seat with all the strength of both hands. And looked backward again.

There he was. Coming off the slope at their back, speeding his horse along. But no longer just keeping apace at a distance.

He was pushing hard, riding to overtake them. He was gaining on them yard by yard.

"Truitt, hurry up!"

Ariel was aware of a pitched scream in her voice. But Truitt needed no urging. His face was set-jawed, pale under its tan. He was as scared as she was. He yelled wildly at the team.

The meadow flats tilted up to a roll of the land, then downward again to another stretch of flats.

The man was a lot closer by now. He didn't seem in a particular hurry. He was merely goading his mount enough to keep overtaking them at a steady pace. The drumming of hooves, the ominous creaking of the old buckboard—as if it might fall to pieces at any moment—battered at Ariel's senses.

She kept looking frenziedly backward. He was easily closing the distance between them. In moments he'd be upon them.

He was nearly close enough for her to make out his face. A big man, long and rawboned. A slouch hat pulled tight and low over his forehead. His clenched teeth showed through his drawn-back lips; his jaws bristled with a black stubble of beard.

His horse. She knew the horse. A blaze-faced sorrel that belonged to her father. Just a few days ago she had seen it ranging loose in the stable pasture.

He was pulling close, closer.

Now he was racing along behind them, pulling over toward the side as though to pass the wagon . . . to head it off? He wore a strange assortment of ragged clothing that streamed out behind him. His eyes glinted like sparks in the shadow of his hat. His teeth shone yellowly. *He was smiling*.

"Truitt!" she shrilled into the wind.

"God damn," he shouted, "I am pushing fast as I—"

A terrific crash and jolt. The left forewheel had hit a rock . . . or something hard and jutting.

That was all Ariel had time to know. Suddenly her hold on the wagon seat was torn away. She felt herself being flipped head over heels in space, the world pinwheeling wildly around her.

She hit the ground with a slamming impact that momentarily stunned her. Next thing she knew was that she was lying belly down, grass and earth mashed against her face. She managed to turn her face sideways, coughing and gagging.

The wagon team was running away at a gallop, trailing the harness and wagontree behind it. A few yards from her the shattered wagon box lay overturned, buckled and splintered. One wheel, freed of its axle, was spinning away from the wreck. She stared at it with a kind of idiotic detachment, watching it start to wobble, then topple on its side.

Ariel coughed and blinked, turning her head farther around.

She saw Truitt just a few feet away. He was pinned under the wreckage of the wagon. Only his head and upper trunk showed. His head was flung back, his face upturned and bloody, and he was motionless.

Ariel clawed her fingers into the shredded turf and pushed up on her hands and knees, still coughing. She heard the rattle of a horse's bit chain above her.

She twisted her head around and backward, squinting upward.

The sun was a blazing aureole behind the dark shape of the man's head and shoulders. She heard the thud of his feet as he dropped to the ground. Saw the boots moving close to her as he bent down. Felt a powerful arm snake around her middle and lift her effortlessly to her feet.

His face was close to hers, gaunt and grinning. Wolflike, the eyes red-rimmed and feral. Ariel screamed once. Then she fainted dead away.

CHAPTER EIGHT

Pᴀʀʀʏ ᴅɪᴅɴ'ᴛ ᴇᴠᴇɴ ᴛʜɪɴᴋ ᴏғ ᴍᴀᴋɪɴɢ ʜɪs ʜᴀsᴛʏ ʀᴇᴛᴜʀɴ to the WP headquarters with his wagon and team.

He went immediately to Vardon's livery barn and asked for "a fast racker"—a saddle mount with real bottom that could get him back home in a hurry. He asked the hostler to put up his own outfit, left in front of the general merchandise store, until he came back for it.

Afterward he lined out on the road east toward WP, pushing the roan as fast he dared.

One of the first things they drummed into you if you'd ever served in the army—even if you weren't cavalry—was that if you had to ride a horse on any mission, no matter how urgent, you weren't to drive the animal too fast or hard. Horses weren't long on endurance. At an all-out run, they might founder in a quarter hour or so.

But Will Parry, with Tom Redfern's telegram burning in his mind, had all he could do not to push the roan ahead for all it was worth. With any luck, he should reach headquarters by mid-afternoon.

It should be all right, he kept telling himself. Leah would be at her usual household work; Ariel would be watching Tim. Truitt and Genardo would be working the horses. Only Linc and Bill Soholt would be out on-range, away from the place. Mast wasn't likely to strike at the headquarters in broad daylight . . . was he? If it was he—not Virg

Bollinger—who'd shot Timmy, he had done it under cover of a snowstorm.

It wasn't Bollinger who had killed the chickens, shot out the windows, almost fatally wounded Tim. Parry had a sickening certainty of it. Bollinger was a drink-addled fool whose single shot at retribution had cost him his life.

Josey Mast was the man. To Parry's mind, Redfern's message had confirmed it with a jolting conviction. And there was no way of predicting Josey Mast. He might do anything. At any time it suited him.

Settling the roan into a steady, driving pace on the road east, not daring to push faster and yet sick with thoughts of what might be happening, Parry felt his mind range back across time. To events that remained unmuddied by time, standing out as vivid as yesterday. . . .

Josey Mast had been born and partly raised in a backwoods country that was vaguely Southern. Nobody was sure just where the family came from. Kentucky or maybe Arkansas. Somewhere out of the backwash of an older frontier, where old grudges were never forgotten, where clan feuds went on for generations. The Masts had settled in northeastern Illinois fifteen or so years before Will and Leah Parry had come there as newlyweds.

The Mast clan had been regarded by the quiet, staid folks of Jo Daviess County and the town of Galena as trash of the worst ilk. Amoral, totally illiterate, fanatically devoted to their own kind, with a vicious inbred suspicion of all outsiders. Nobody was sure just why the large, loosely related clan had migrated north. Rumor had it that authorities had run them out of their home country for operating forbidden distilleries, getting illegitimate offspring on their sisters, bushwhacking neighbors over slight disagreements, and God knew what all.

Young Josey Mast had had a reputation as one of the

worst of the lot even before he'd enlisted in Ulysses "Sam" Grant's company of militia volunteers at the outbreak of war in early '61. That was when and where he and Will Parry had first met and clashed.

Will was already a sergeant by the time Grant's volunteers were absorbed into the 21st Illinois Infantry. Josey Mast, serving in Parry's outfit, had been a pain in the ass from the first. If he wasn't in one sort of trouble, he was in another. Taking off for a drunk or a brawl, going absent without leave to visit his degenerate relatives, whatever. He was promoted to corporal and then broken back to private four different times.

Over and over, Will Parry had gone out of his way to take Mast's part, urging Sam Grant and other superiors to be patient with the man's idiosyncrasies. When he wasn't off on some crazy bat, Mast was an invaluable member of the company. Down south, isolated in near-wilderness hill country, his kinfolk had honed their woods-wise abilities to a superb edge. After coming north, they'd continued their old way of life in the rugged and wooded country around Galena, which was an exception to the usual flat prairie lands of Illinois.

Josey Mast's woodcraft was uncanny. When it came to making a lone reconnaissance behind enemy lines or heading up an unorthodox guerilla sortie of some kind on an enemy position, Mast was unbeatable.

Far from being grateful for Parry's interventions on his behalf, Mast, with the perverse nature of his kind, had cultivated a smoldering resentment toward his sergeant. It had quickly grown to an unconcealed hatred.

Everything between them had come to a head during the long, bitter, drawn-out siege of Vicksburg. It had lasted from the spring of 1862 to the Fourth of July 1863, when Grant was finally victorious.

If Vicksburg were taken, the Confederacy would effectively be cut in half. Knowing it, the Confederates had laid out strong fortifications at this vital point on the Mississippi River. They successfully defended them against Grant's attempt to move on their defenses by land from Memphis and Grand Junction while Sherman attacked from the river side. They also succeeded temporarily in smashing Grant's lines of supply and communication. He was losing his reputation for effective leadership.

By the late spring of 1863 Grant was easily receptive to an idea put forth by Will Parry, now a company captain who also functioned as liaison with Grant's personal staff. Parry suggested that the Union troops supplement their artillery and rifle fire by tunneling under a key fortification. They could place a charge of powder that would be timed to go off after the party of sappers had made a hasty withdrawal.

With Grant's full approval, Parry assigned Sergeant Sean Mulhare to head up a patrol of several seasoned troopers, including Private Josey Mast. They were constantly to reconnoiter the heavily wooded area where the tunnel digging would commence—forward of the lines and somewhat north of them. It was a fairly secluded place, but one on which some Confederate sympathizer, maybe a snipe hunter or a stray berry picker, might innocently stumble and uncover the tunneling activity. So it was crucial that any such person or persons be captured or, barring any other recourse, shot if necessary to maintain secrecy.

Parry remembered the sodden, dripping day when Sean Mulhare had approached the headquarters tent where he was composing a report on the operation for Grant. The beefy, red-faced noncom had snapped a shaky salute.

"Begging the captain's pardon," Mulhare said. "I'm afraid I've the grimmest sort of news for your ears." His voice broke a little. "Jasus, sir. Jasus and the Blessed Virgin and all the saints."

The two of them passed the sentry lines and tramped

through the steady whisper of falling rain to a clearing back in the dense trees. Here Corporal Tom Redfern and two other men were holding Josey Mast, muskets trained on him. Mast, a huge, rawboned, and gauntly powerful man, fully six inches over six feet in height, stood with arms folded, grinning wolfishly through his black beard without a trace either of fear or regret in his manner.

And he wasn't drunk. He was stark sober, calmly accepting the discovery of what he'd done. Utterly contemptuous of his captors and whatever consequences he might face.

What Mast had done, while out on reconnaissance by himself, was come across a trio of local girls, all in their mid-teens, on a huckleberry gathering party. Terrifying them into submission, he had tied up all three girls and begun to do things to them.

"*Unspeakable* things, sir," Mulhare said in a trembling voice. Corporal Redfern, a taciturn and seldom-spoken man, only nodded agreement. So did the other soldiers. But all of them looked a little sick.

Luckily for the girls, Redfern had happened on the scene before Mast had gone too far. Holding Mast at bay with a musket, he'd shouted loud enough to bring Mulhare and the others to the spot.

It had seemed all right to let the girls go free. Though none was really harmed, they were frightened half out of their wits, hysterical and weeping, begging to go home to their folks. They knew nothing about the sapping operation, only that they'd been surprised by some Union scouts. Then Mulhare had gone at once to fetch Captain Parry.

Standing in the gray drizzle of rain, Parry dismally considered Mulhare's unspoken question: Could this be excused as easily as Mast's other derelictions? After questioning Mulhare and Redfern and the others on the details of what Mast had been about, he decided it was necessary to bring Private Josey Mast to court-martial. To face imprisonment or a firing squad; whatever was decreed for him.

But a military court-martial was a tricky piece of business. Mast was extraordinarily lucky in getting Major Josiah Lamprey as his defense counsel. Lamprey was shrewd and zealous and had visions of a lucrative postwar legal practice. Mast's would make a good practice case. An accused enlisted man had the right to demand that at least one-third of the membership of the general or special court-martial that heard his case be composed of enlisted personnel from his own company. Major Lamprey managed to maneuver onto the court-martial panel a couple of enlisted men who—unknown to trial counsel and practically everyone else—weren't far from Mast's own degenerate bent.

Along with Lamprey's brilliant presentation of the case, that was enough to ensure that Josey Mast received nothing worse than a "bad conduct discharge" from the United States Army.

It was a bitter blow to the trial counsel, to Will Parry and Sean Mulhare and Tom Redfern and the other two witnesses. Under other circumstances, Mast might have received the death penalty for the atrocity he had seemed about to carry through.

Josey Mast's depraved or sadistic or insane tendencies, call them what you would, hadn't caught up with him until a year and a half later. Invalided home late in 1864 after losing an arm at Petersburg, Will Parry was still recovering from his amputation when he was summoned to testify at a civil court action in Galena.

Mast had been brought to docket for the alleged rape-murder of a fourteen-year-old girl, Priscilla Evans. The evidence against him was strong but highly circumstantial. It was the testimony of Parry and Mulhare and Redfern—

the other two soldier witnesses to the tableau outside Vicksburg having since been killed in action—that had tipped the
scales against Mast this time.

Almost at once the jury brought in a verdict of guilty and
Judge John T. Venner sentenced Mast to life imprisonment
in the state prison outside of Joliet, Illinois. Raising his
voice to a kind of calm, unexcited roar—just enough to be
heard above the courtroom hubbub—Mast had made his
vow of revenge.

Joliet's well-guarded stone walls had contained Josey
Mast for sixteen years. And now, according to Redfern's
telegram, Mast had escaped. The why and how didn't
matter. Sean Mulhare and Judge Venner were dead. That
alone told Will Parry as much as he needed to know.

All of the memories rushed back on Parry with the force
of certainty as he sped back toward WP headquarters.
Strongest were his vivid-as-yesterday memories of Mast
himself. His uncanny woodcraft. His brute animal power
and cunning and patience. His amoral and frightening
hungers.

Most of all, his particular and obsessive hatred for one
man who had been his superior in the war. . . .

CHAPTER NINE

COMING OFF THE LAST SWELL OF HILLY GROUND JUST WEST of the headquarters layout, Parry felt a brief lift of relief.

From a couple hundred yards away, everything looked placid under the mid-afternoon sun. The two-storied house and the sprawl of outbuildings seemed to drowse like a pack of sleepy dogs. Nothing out of the ordinary . . . except that a pale funnel of smoke rising from the kitchen smokestack indicated that Leah had chosen today, a day earlier than her usual once-a-week bakeday, to prepare the dense, nutty-tasting bread that was served at every meal.

Swinging out of his saddle in front of the house, Parry glanced toward the corrals and saw no sign of horsebreaking activity. That was unusual. Ordinarily Genardo would still have Truitt working the mustangs at this hour. Tramping into the house, though, he was reassured by the sight of his wife.

A rich odor of baking bread filled the kitchen. Leah was stooped down in front of the open door of the oven, peering inside to check on her loaves. She looked up with a startled smile.

"Will! You're back so early. . . ."

"Everything all right?"

Leah closed the oven door and straightened up, her face sobering at the sight of his. "Why . . . I suppose. What could be wrong?"

97

Parry said grimly, "A whole lot, maybe," and told her in a few spare words, seeing the color drain from her face.

"Oh my God," she whispered. "Josey Mast. *Will* . . ."

"Lee, has anything happened *here*, today? That's what I—"

"No—no!" She was staring at him, crumpling the cloth of her apron between her hands. "But Ariel went out for a ride . . . with Truitt. . . ."

It took just seconds to get what he needed to know out of his terrified wife. Then Parry was wheeling out of the kitchen, plunging down the porch steps, grabbing up the reins of the roan.

Heading eastward for the stable pasture, he made no effort to hold the animal in. A swarm of fears chased through his mind. Overriding everything else was his memory of Mast's predilection for young girls. And what Alder Kane had told him this morning, about the disappearance of a young prostitute.

His depredations so far indicated that Mast was in no hurry to wreak retribution on the main object of his revenge, Will Parry. He meant to drag out a deadly war of nerves on the man he hated most. Whittling Parry down by degrees. Going at him through his family. Tim had been chosen as the first victim.

But *Ariel*! His daughter on the ripening edge of womanhood . . . out away from the relative safety of their home. Under the doubtful protection of Truitt Barrows. Both of them ignorant of any danger.

Angry questions flickered through Parry's brain. When had Mast made his escape? It must have been some time back. For he'd had time to learn where Will Parry was living, make his way out to Wyoming, then patiently reconnoiter and size up the country—Mast would do that—before making his first move.

God—and Tom didn't get to letting me know till now!

But it wasn't hard to figure why.

Tom Redfern, a very young corporal in his wartime company, had since become a bounty hunter in the West, tracking down wanted men for the rewards on their heads. Alder Kane had once told Parry as much, when Redfern's name had come up by chance in conversation. Redfern's work would take him on long and exhausting quests during which he'd be out of touch with everything for weeks, maybe months at a time. All the same, Redfern had connections with law officers all over the West. Once he'd touched home base again, it was sure he'd been quick to pick up on Mast. And he'd swiftly have been able to find out, if he didn't already know, where Will Parry was now.

Redfern had done what he could manage to do at once— send a warning telegram to Chinook Basin. He was coming here as fast as he could. *And maybe we'll all be dead when he gets here!*

These thoughts flickered in and out of Parry's mind. All he could fix on now was overtaking Ariel and Truitt.

The thawed earth and new grass of the stable pasture showed the mashed ruts of the old buckboard's wheels. Their twin ribbons led almost straight east. The terrain was upsloping, mostly open flats, a little bumpy but easily negotiable. Parry could only pray they hadn't gone too far . . . or had turned back by now.

He realized he was driving the roan horse too hard. Its flanks were lathered and laboring against the press of his knees. Ahead was a shallow rise where he could halt and give the roan a few moments of rest, and not really lose any time. He'd have a long view of the rolling grassy landscape, right up to the wooded base of the Buckhorn Hills. Taking in the sweep of open country ahead, and to the left and right, he might quickly spot the buckboard somewhere on the meadows and actually save himself some time.

Coming atop the rise, Parry saw the buckboard at once—

but with a rush of terror that held him momentarily paralyzed.

From this distance, hundreds of yards away, it was as if he were watching a tableau of antlike figures performing a puppet play of sorts. He could make it out clearly. The buckboard was lurching its way across the flats, a lone rider not far behind it. Then the wagon was veering suddenly to the side, overturning.

Parry kicked the roan into motion. He poured off the rise in an unheeding run.

Pounding toward the scene, he saw all that happened next. Saw it with a chilling clarity and, because he was much too far away to prevent any of it, with an aching sense of helplessness.

The wagon had overturned, but one of the occupants was thrown clear. It was Ariel. He made out the flutter of her skirt as she was pitched to the ground.

The lone rider was pulling up now, swinging down and moving over to her, seizing her up and carrying her back to his horse. Mounted again, with Ariel flung across the saddle in front of him, he turned his horse back toward the Buckhorns. In moments he achieved the lower slopes and was vanishing into the trees.

Parry passed the runaway buckboard team and the trailing wagontree. He raced on, slowing only for a moment as he came abreast of the upended buckboard. Truitt was pinned beneath it, bloody-faced and unmoving. He might be unconscious or he might be dead. Badly hurt, for sure. Parry's hesitation was brief. He kicked the slobbering roan onward, aware that it was on the edge of foundering.

God . . . *what else could he do?* With his daughter in the hands of Josey Mast.

The worst terror he'd ever known filled Will Parry's mind. He drove ahead and came onto the forested slopes and sent the roan scrambling up the twisting switchbacks of the old trail.

He wondered if he and Mast had distantly spotted each other at about the same time. Even if Mast had seen him, it hadn't prevented him from coolly taking the time to grab up Ariel. *If he did spot me, he'll push all the faster.* Yet Mast's horse would be bearing a double burden and that would slow him some. At the same time Parry could feel the roan's stride starting to break. The animal couldn't last much longer. . . .

By now the trees were crowded so dense and close to the climbing trail that he couldn't make out anything beyond the next bend. But he heard a faint and frightened cry. That was Ariel. And he was close upon them, Parry knew then, closer than he'd dared hope.

A quick twist of the trail and there they were—God!—no more than a couple hundred feet ahead of him. Parry's eyes were blurred with a sting of sweat. But he registered everything in a fleeting instant.

Josey Mast twisting in his saddle to look backward. Bearded, with a battered hat pulled nearly low enough to hide his face, but his big rawboned form instantly recognizable. Ariel half-hidden from sight, thrown facedown across the horse's withers in front of Mast, held down but furiously kicking and struggling. And the broad sorrel rump of the horse itself—one of his own mustangs, Parry detachedly realized.

Parry let go of his reins to fumble for the Colt revolver holstered at his left side.

Mast turned his head to glance forward, bent down for a moment, then reared up and looked back again, yelling at the top of his voice. Parry couldn't make out his hoarse, taunting words. But a moment later Ariel was tumbling sideways from in front of Mast, flung away like a rag doll.

Mast, his pace unbroken, was speeding on, hunched deep

across the sorrel's neck. Almost at once he swerved around another bend in the trail. Briefly Parry traced his flight through the thinning trees beyond.

Then Mast was gone, lost to sight.

Parry slowed his horse and pulled it to a blubbering stop beside Ariel. She had fallen on a mat of dead leaves by the trail and lay on her back, coughing and sobbing.

He dropped to the ground and knelt by her, pulling her up in his arms. Her hands clasped behind his neck and her fingers convulsively closed and opened as she sobbed weakly. On his knees, holding her, Parry rocked her gently back and forth as he hadn't in years, not since she was a small girl and had run to him to be comforted for some childish hurt.

"Daddy . . ." She found her voice at last, but choked on the words. "Daddy, he said . . ."

"It's all right, baby. Don't try to talk."

Ariel gave her head a violent shake, her red hair whipping from side to side. She was crying, but not hysterically. Her eyes shone blue and bright and angry through her tears.

"He said to tell you he will be seeing you. To tell you . . . he'll have me in hand again, too."

He'll be in hell before that happens. The thought skimmed only the surface of Parry's mind. Holding his daughter close, saying only calming words, he was aware that the chilling fear in him hadn't abated at all.

He kept his good arm around Ariel's shoulders as they walked back across the flats to the overturned buckboard. The roan's bridle was looped over the hook of his other arm. The animal was still blubbering softly, head lowered. But he hadn't foundered and the best thing now was to walk him slowly.

With a crawling sensation between his shoulder blades as he went, Parry looked back often at the wooded slopes. Be damned easy for Josey Mast to draw a bead on them if he wanted to circle back and shoot them down from cover of the trees.

But it wouldn't come that swiftly or easily, Parry could now be sure.

Mast hadn't relinquished his designs on Ariel. He'd abandoned her just now only so he wouldn't be overtaken. Mast would continue to work around Will Parry, striking at him through the people he cared about most. He'd drag it out as long as possible. Inflict all the anguish he could on a hated enemy before ending it for good.

We'll see, Parry thought grimly.

Ariel was trembling in the circle of his arm, weeping quietly. She kept rubbing at her tear-streaked face, but she was in control of herself.

"Daddy," she whispered. "Truitt . . . ?"

Parry said nothing. Just tightened his arm and shook his head in negation once, side to side. And then they were standing beside the buckboard, the whole rig crumpled and smashed in its sudden overturning.

Truitt was dead. No doubt of it, now that Parry had the time to bend down and examine the body. Before, in his confused haste, he hadn't really registered the fact that Truitt's head lolled sideways at a grotesque angle. He must have been killed almost instantly. His neck might have been broken even before the wagon's buckled weight had come down on his lower trunk, crushing it.

"This was . . . all my . . . fault," Ariel choked. "If I just hadn't . . ."

Parry said roughly, "Quit that now." He hugged her against his chest as she wept out her grief and her self-blame.

But it was going to be with her for a long time, he knew. It was going to stick on all of them, like burrs under a saddle blanket, for a long, long time. Whatever else they might have thought about him, Truitt had been one of them in a way. One of their own. And he had died accidentally and senselessly.

For he hadn't been one of the targets of Josey Mast's revenge. Truitt had just happened to be in the way at the wrong time.

CHAPTER TEN

Parry and Ariel started back on foot to WP headquarters, leading the winded roan. They were halfway across the stable pasture when Linc and Bill Soholt, riding from the other direction, met them. The two had come in from the day's work and, learning the latest development from Leah, had lost no time in following Parry up. It was decided that Parry and Soholt would go back and extricate Truitt's body from under the broken-up buckboard and bring it home, while Linc and Ariel continued to headquarters on foot. They'd be in the open all the way, nobody could steal up on them, and Linc had his rifle. . . .

That evening they all sat around the table and discussed what had to be done.

Leah dished up a sketchy supper of sorts, for which nobody had much appetite. The shock of Truitt's death, and the bleak fear of what they still might have to face, threw a sobering shadow over the talk.

Parry's mind was already made up. He and his family must evacuate the ranch and move to town. He didn't have to impress upon any of them the threat that Mast, on the loose and savagely unpredictable in his actions, posed to them all. Way out here, isolated from the comparative protection that even a small settlement of people might offer, they were pitifully vulnerable.

"That sounds right as rain," agreed Bill Soholt. "Me and

Genardo can hold the place down for a spell. You folks get to Salvation and stick there till this Mast is brought to ground."

Genardo nodded his white head vigorously. "*Sí.* Tha's what we will do, *patrón.*"

Parry's objection was half-hearted. Privately, he knew Bill was right. Everything they owned was bound up in this outfit. Somebody had to stay on and look after things, tend to livestock and keep the work going. But, he said aloud, he couldn't ask either man to take that risk.

"You don't need to ask," Soholt told him. "Look, Will, you said it. It's you and yours he's out to get. Genardo and me don't count with him. He won't go after us."

"That's a guess on my part," Parry said wearily. "Suppose he took it in his head to fire this place? Every damn building on it? Or pick off the cattle and horses? Not much else one man can do to a working ranch. But he could do that. If he tried and you were in the way . . ."

"All the more reason us two should stay on," Soholt said stubbornly. "Damn it, Will. Don't you go belaboring this, now. Old-timers like Genardo and me, we taken plenty chances in our time. So have you. It's a man's lot. I never turned tail from a duty in my life. A man's beholden to his hire and his brand. And I reckon this is our home, too." He paused. "I don't need to tell you your duty. It's to look after your own flesh and blood. You do it."

"All right, Bill." Parry rubbed a hand over his face, shaking his head a little. "All right."

Linc was sitting with his arms tightly folded, silent and brooding, staring at his plate. Parry had a pretty good idea of what was going through his son's mind, and he said gently, "Linc?"

Linc said, "Yes, Pa?" Not looking up.

"You're thinking you ought to stay on here, too. Along

with Bill and Genardo. Help watch over things. Am I right?"

Linc raised his eyes, locking his father's gaze. "I ain't a kid any more, Pa. I don't need to go to town and have you looking over me like a mother hen. With Ma and Ariel and Tim, that's okay. That's fine. But I want to be of some use. I'll go along with whatever's your say-so—" He straightened up in his chair, balled a fist, and dropped it on the table. "But damn it, Pa, I can't just sit around and do nothing! I know you won't. It wouldn't be like you. You got something more than that in mind. I want to be in on it."

Parry nodded, half-smiling. But in a wry and dour way. "You're right. I wish I could keep you out of it, Linc. But you wouldn't stand for it. And I don't want you going off half-cocked on your own. All right. This is what I have in mind to do. . . ."

None of his thinking had anything to do with any actual defense of the buildings and livestock. How much could be done, after all? Soholt and Genardo could stay alert, stick close to headquarters, and go armed at all times. Barney would be on hand to raise an alarm at any intrusion.

Early next morning, Parry lashed Truitt's body onto the livery roan and made a five-mile ride to take the dead boy and his meager belongings home to his folks, who had a small outfit north of WP. The Barrowses, outside of Truitt, were a withdrawn and inhospitable lot. But this much, at least, Parry considered to be his own bounden duty. He gave them his best condolences, briefly endured the lamentations of Truitt's mother and sisters and the stony-eyed silence of Truitt's pa and younger brother, then awkwardly took his leave.

From there he rode to Salvation, left the roan at the livery barn, claimed his own spring wagon and team, and got back to headquarters in a hurry.

They loaded some necessary supplies and clothes and other gear that would be useful for a protracted stay in town into the wagon, with Tim nested in a cocoon of blankets behind the seat. Other things could be fetched in later if they were needed. After saying good-byes to Soholt and Genardo, and giving them a final needless warning, he handed Leah up to the high seat of the wagon, climbed up beside her, and set the team in motion. Linc and Ariel rode behind the wagon, and Linc led a string of three spare horses.

Reaching town by mid-afternoon, they drove straight to Alder Kane's house. The sheriff was up and around, moving kind of gingerly but with a good color in his face, and still champing at the bit (against his wife's protests) to get back on the job. After learning of Truitt's fate, and what else had happened, Kane agreed with Parry's plan to set up a guard of volunteers to protect his family. Also to organize a posse of seasoned men into an all-out effort to hunt down Josey Mast.

"And how," demanded Kate Kane, "will you folks be making out in town without a roof over your heads? Surely you'll not be putting up at the Hammond House, Will Parry? It's a fleabag of a hostelry at best and that Henry Hammond charges ungodly rates."

"No," said Parry. "I thought we might set up a tent on a vacant lot. . . ."

"You'll do no such thing. We've a great barn of a house, Alder and me, that's mostly a lot of empty rooms since all our kids are gone. You and your family can be occupying those."

Alder Kane firmly seconded his wife's suggestion, and Parry made only a token objection. The frame house would afford far better shelter and protection than a tent, and it could easily be guarded by a couple of men. The Parrys and their possessions were promptly moved into the house.

Parry and Linc carried Tim up to the second floor and installed him in a comfortable bed.

While Kate helped Leah and Ariel get settled in, and Linc put up their horses in a stable at the rear, Alder Kane took Parry aside and told him a startling piece of news. Maybelle, the child prostitute who had disappeared from Horrid Hattie's, had been found. Or rather, she had straggled in by herself yesterday morning, shortly after Parry had made his hasty departure from Salvation.

Parry said incredulously, "And she wasn't . . . she didn't come to any harm?"

"Well"—Kane brushed a finger across the tips of his mustache—"not by *her* way of reckoning. But she had a story that makes a little sense . . . maybe. You want to amble over to Hattie's with me, you can get it all straight from Maybelle herself."

The two of them left the house, crossed the tracks, and presented themselves at the door of Harriet's Boarding Academy.

Mrs. Harriet Outram, or Horrid Hattie, answered their knock. She was a plump, grandmotherly sort of woman who wore her gray hair in a tight bun, blinked pleasantly behind steel-rimmed spectacles, and acknowledged Kane's introduction of Will Parry. She comfortably observed that it was real funny he'd never come in, a big strapping fellow like him.

Parry's face was burning with discomfort as Mrs. Outram ushered them into a fairly lavish parlor or waiting room and seated them on a plush sofa. Wasn't it a dreadful warm day and would they care for some cold lemonade? No? Well, it had been a dreadful long night, what with so many boys coming in off winter range, and the girls were just now rousting out. Exiting through a doorway hung with red velour drapes, Horrid Hattie added over her shoulder that

Maybelle would be in here directly and she was a real dear but you had to be patient-like with her.

Alder Kane couldn't help chuckling at his companion's sweating discomfiture. "Ever stray into the beat of that lady before, Will?"

"No, sir." Parry swiped a bandanna over his face. "Not even back when I was a whole lot younger and a lot more foolish."

Kane laughed.

Presently Maybelle came through the velour drapes. She was a skinny, straw-haired little thing with a cheerfully vapid expression. Kane greeted her kindly and told her to repeat everything she'd told him yesterday. Well, said Maybelle, she had gone out to catch some night air between tricks and she was grabbed from behind and a hand clapped over her mouth and she was carried off into a willow thicket down by the river. At Kane's prompting, she told what her captor looked like—there was a big round moon out and she could see him plainly—and her description of him, crude as it was, made his identity unmistakable.

Josey Mast.

Parry said so, and Alder Kane raised an eyebrow at him. "Anything *you* want to ask about, Will?"

"Well—" Parry hunched forward uncomfortably. "Miss—uh, Maybelle, what did he do exactly? I mean, he didn't do you any harm. . . ."

Maybelle tittered nasally. "Laws, no, mister. We *done* just 'bout ever'thing, you know? But he didn't hurt me none. He was real easy with me and it was kind of fun even and then I felt real t'ared and I sort of went off to sleep. Didn't wake up till near noon and there I was all snugged up in this ol' coat he left me wrapped in and I jus' got up and come back to Miz Outram's."

Kane cleared his throat. "What else did he leave with you, Maybelle?"

"Oh, this here." Maybelle reached in the pocket of her frowsy wrapper and held out a twenty-dollar gold piece. "A gen-u-wine double eagle! I ain't never got the like before from a gent, just for hardly anything atall."

The two men left Horrid Hattie's and headed back across the tracks. Alder Kane said mildly, "That was something, eh?"

Parry shook his head dismally, his jaw knotted. "Al . . . that poor kid. She's not even as old as my girl. Jesus Christ."

"All right, Will. I know how you feel. But Maybelle's alive and well . . . as well as she'll ever be. Like you said about this Mast, he fancies 'em young. But he wouldn't treat you or yours so lightly. Proved that with your boy Tim. Reckon it tots up like you figured. He's just out to fetch *you*."

"Yes."

Kane rubbed his chin slowly. "And he's been stealing for his needs. Took a couple of your chickens. And that sorrel of yours. And a saddle and bridle from somewhere. Don't know where he lifted that gold piece . . . but Clevenger's store was busted into last night and there was quite a few things taken. Some jerky, crackers, beans, dried apples, stuff he can store up. Some blankets and a tarp. And a coil of wire. If it was Mast, seems like he aims to settle down for a spell. Bide his time."

But where? Parry thought wildly. Where in hell is he hiding out?

Tom Redfern had sent word he was coming to Chinook Basin as fast he could make it. But he hadn't arrived yet, and Parry had no intention of waiting for him. Not with his family in mortal danger.

With Alder Kane's help, he lost no time in sounding out townsmen who might be willing to assist him in running

Mast to ground. These men were merchants or clerks or craftsmen or swampers, but they weren't just a passel of soft-bellied counterjumpers. They were bred-to-the-bone Western men, most of them. Many had been soldiers in the war (on one side or the other), Indian fighters, miners, stage drivers, ranchhands, or whatever, in their time. When one of their own was in trouble, they could be counted on to help him out. Some volunteered to ride to outlying ranches in the Basin and recruit others.

By evening of the next day, a sizeable number of men had agreed to serve on the posse. Ranchers, their sons, their hired hands. Others were reluctant to join up because the spring roundup was keeping them tied down.

Mostly, those who held back were concerned about their families, fearing that with a crazy ridge-runner like Mast on the loose, their first duty was to stay home and watch over their own. Some townsmen felt the same way. Even so, a posse of nearly fifty men showed up the following morning in front of Alder Kane's house, mounted and well-armed.

Parry and the sheriff had already arranged for a watch to be kept on Kane's house. Two men would be stationed at positions that were well apart. Each would be situated at a strategic angle from which he could command a full view of two sides of the place. Nobody could steal up on any side without being spotted. The guard duty would be rotated every four hours. Men who wouldn't go out on posse for one reason or another were willing to take on a guard shift.

One of them was Nils Nansen.

At last Nils had worked up a satisfactory version of the "contraption" that would replace the hook on Parry's arm. He showed it to Parry in the morning, as the posse was assembling.

"Can't hold a saddle with this damn pegleg of mine," declared Nils. "But by *Gud*, I can help stand the watch right here. And the contraption, Will, you will be able to shoot a rifle with it! Look here—"

It was quite a dingus, sure enough: short, hollow iron cylinder full of slots and clamps and brackets that, strapped to the stump of Parry's right arm, could be fitted with ordinary tools or utensils that would enable him to do almost anything a two-handed man could do.

Parry gazed at the device, nodding with a slow and mounting bewilderment as he listened to Nils expound on all the mechanics of it. "That's quite a thing, all right," he managed to say.

Big Nils rumbled a chuckle. "You and me, we make between us a good man-and-a-half as to limbs, eh? But now you will do as well as a whole man."

"Mm." Parry was still nodding gently. "You know what, Nils? You ought to work up something for your leg, too. I bet if you put your mind to it, you could come up with something better than just a wood peg—"

"By *Gud*!" An explosion of inspired delight lit up Nils's broad face. "Ain't it a funny thing, I never thought of *that* before! I bet I can, too. I will go to work on it, Will!"

Alder Kane had wanted to go out with the posse, but had grudgingly yielded to the combined arguments of his wife and Parry and Doc Costiner. Stricken by one serious heart attack (as he now admitted it to be), Kane conceded that the arduous demands of posse duty were no longer for him.

Parry would head up the operation, and his first act of command was to split the assembled men into five separate groups. Each was to cover a specific section of the Basin, its hills and flats, meadows and timber. All these men knew the country like the seams of their own palms, and there was no need to give them other than general instructions.

Each party was assigned a leader and a man to scout trail. In two cases, these were the same men. In two other cases, Parry had to be more politic. A party of whites wouldn't accept the leadership of old Benjy, Horrid Hattie's colored man-of-all-chores, but everyone readily granted his qualifications as an ex–army scout. Big Bear, a Cheyenne of Little Crow's band, was acceptable as a tracker second to none in Chinook Basin, but no white man was about to take orders from an "Injun."

For the party Parry would head up himself, Linc would serve as scout. Linc wouldn't be kept out of the doings and this way, at least, Parry had the assurance of keeping his son at his side. There were several other father-son teams present, and Parry made a point of seeing each of them assigned to the same group.

Afterward he tramped over to the porch where Alder Kane was standing, hands jammed in his pockets, smiling in a wry and half-sardonic way.

"Al," Parry said, "I can't handle this business any way close to how you would. But I'll do my damnedest."

"I know you will. That ain't what's galling me." Kane pulled his right hand from his pocket and gripped Parry's only hand. "You'll do fine. Good luck, son."

The parties of men mounted up and split apart and headed out.

Just east of town, after crossing the bridge over the Blackbow, Parry began fiddling with Nils's "contraption," now strapped to his stump. It was an awkward and alien weight on his wrist and he couldn't really make head or tail of it. After a couple minutes, swearing softly to himself, he stripped off the dingus, jammed it in his saddlebag, and replaced it with his own leather-jacketed hook.

The hunt went badly from the start. Whatever else might be said of Josey Mast, he was more than a match for the best they could put up against him.

On the first day they cut no sign of him at all. On the second day two of the parties crossed track that had to be

Mast's. They found prints of the sorrel he'd lifted from Will Parry's stable pasture—easily identified by a built-up caulk in the shoe of the right forehoof—but each time the sign petered out on rocky terrain.

On the third day two other parties, one of them Parry's, actually caught three glimpses of Mast through field glasses. Each time he was so far away that even Parry could identify only the sorrel horse that he sat on. Always Mast was looking their way, fully aware of being watched. Each time he lifted a hand in an insouciant salute, then faded away into cover. Each time, when they reached the spot, they were unable to pick up his track beyond a few hundred feet.

At each day's end, the tired and grumbling men would gather back at Alder Kane's house to swap experiences and grouse about the situation in general. This son of a bitch was playing an easy and savagely contemptuous game with them. It was like chasing a ghost.

Parry himself had the sinking conviction that Mast could drag things out forever if he chose. Back in the war he'd displayed almost a preternatural instinct for anticipating an enemy's movements. Not in any formally strategic or tactical way, certainly. But on any sort of natural terrain, he had a cunning and foresight that went far beyond a normal man's instincts or training. The best of their scouts couldn't remotely match him in the field, alone or in teams.

More complaints of casual depredations began to dribble in. Small articles turned up missing from a wide scatter of places, both in town and at Basin ranches. Sometimes a family dog would give the alarm, but always the intruder was gone like a shadow, taking what he wanted from shelves or pantries or storage sheds. Since Mast's woodcraft would easily enable him to live off the countryside alone, these small thefts were only a way of thumbing his nose at all of them.

He had no particular vendetta against anyone but Will Parry and he was in no hurry. Just dragging out his war of nerves.

Clell Tannit, a testy old misanthrope of a trapper who lived far back in the hills, paid one of his rare visits to town for supplies and fumed about a saddle and bridle that had been stolen from his tack shed a week ago. A relic of an older frontier, a woodsman born and bred, Clell was hopping mad. Not so much about the loss as from his own inability to pick up the thief's trail.

The most alarming report of theft came from an upvalley rancher who was missing a case of dynamite he'd bought to blast out an irrigation ditch to his alfalfa field through a rocky ridge that blocked access to a main stream.

What in God's name did Mast want with dynamite? The possibilities were terrifying.

Men began to drop out of the posses, disgusted and discouraged, or out of pure anxiety. Mast had committed no really harrowing act against any of them, their households, or their holdings, but only because he chose not to. No use inviting it. Stick close to home and protect your own.

The one man Parry thought might have a chance of heading off Mast, of outguessing him on his own terms, was Tom Redfern. Tom had been a damned fine scout himself. Not the equal of Mast, but in the years since the war he'd probably honed his abilities much finer. Alder Kane, a straitlaced lawman who ordinarily had no use for bounty hunters, had the highest respect for Redfern.

But Tom hadn't yet fulfilled his promise of coming to help. Maybe he'd run into an unavoidable delay of one kind or another. But they couldn't just sit on their butts and wait, Parry thought doggedly. They had to keep trying. . . .

CHAPTER ELEVEN

On the morning of the fourth day, sizing up his thinned-out force, Parry suggested a fresh strategy. If Mast again showed himself to any party, the men were to break apart and spread out in a line, beat out and around through brush and timber, try to cordon him off and drive him into a corner. It was a desperate hope, and it came off about as he'd expected.

Parry's own party did spot Mast that day. They tried the maneuver, only to have Mast evade them with chilling ease. They came up with nothing at all and, as usual, Mast simply faded out of sight and left no track whatsoever.

By then it was drawing toward late afternoon. Parry, as disgusted as any of them, agreed they might as well call it quits for the day.

One grizzled old-timer shook his head bleakly. "That sonbitch ain't a man. He's a lobo wolf. He's got the Injun sign on us. I'm almost of a mind to pull out of this."

Parry said, "Never thought I'd hear the like of that from you, Mart. You were poison-baiting wolves before some of us were born."

"Uh-huh," said Mart Willing. "But this 'un's got a man brain. If I was an Injun, now, I'd swear he's somep'n more'n a wolf *or* a man."

Linc, lounging in his saddle, hands crossed on the pommel, smiled just a little. "Like a *nagual*, maybe?"

"What'n hell is that, younker?"

Catching his father's eye, Linc said, "Nothin'. A joke. Forget it."

Parry had given him a warning look. He didn't want these men getting more spooked than they were. So far they were only nerve-frazzled. When someone began talking "Injun sign," they were edging into a realm of superstitious bullshit that lodged close to the surface of every man's unconscious, whether he'd admit it or not.

And none of these men were what Alder Kane had called "soft-bellied counterjumpers." By now the posses had been stripped of their dross. The men who were still hanging in were the toughest breed of backwoods individualists, stubborn as hell. In making fools of them, easily giving them the slip time and again, Mast had stung their pride hard.

None of them was quite ready to give up yet. None voiced the thought that must have been weighing on each of them more and more strongly: that this was Will Parry's trouble, not theirs, and that they'd volunteered themselves into more than they could rightly handle.

They agreed to rendezvous at Alder Kane's the next morning. Then they broke up to head back to town or to their own outfits.

Parry's own range lay inside the swath of country he'd allotted to his group of men to cover. At least once each day he'd seen to it that they swung close to WP headquarters to make sure all was well. A couple times on-range, they'd encountered Bill Soholt, who'd assured them that everything was fine as frog's hair.

Now, with a spell of daylight remaining, and since they hadn't yet checked things out at headquarters in any detail for going on five days, Parry decided he and Linc would cut southward across country to the place and do just that.

The two of them rode in silence for a while, Parry occupied with his grim thoughts. Finally Linc said mildly, "Could be we're going about this the wrong way, Pa."

"Like how?"

"He ain't going to come in range of no posse guns. A couple men, maybe, could smoke him out."

Parry raised a brow, saying dryly, "Like you and me?"

"It's a thought. We two could go on the hunt together. Try him out at his own game. He can easy get wind of a whole bunch of men. That ain't no trick. Could do it myself. But I lay odds that just you and me could . . ."

"Hold up." They pulled their horses to a halt and Parry looked him coldly in the eye. "Told you before. I won't have you taking off alone."

"No. You and me together, though—"

"No," Parry said flatly. "You're good, boy. But he's the best. And I'm no real woodsman any way you cut it. You don't know Josey Mast the way I do."

"I got a pretty fair idea by now," Linc said.

"Then you ought to see we might as well hand him a loaded gun and tell him to do a job on us."

Linc sighed. "All right, Pa. You say not, that's how it'll be. But we're getting no place and we never will, way we're goin' about it."

Parry held a bitter and stubborn silence as they rode on. The boy was right. But so was he. It was like being closed in the jaws of a vise that was winding tight, always tighter. What else could they do? Bring in a crew of "regulators," troubleshooters for hire? Send for troops from the garrison at Fort Wachuca? Either way, what difference would it make?

Men could go on beating the brush till kingdom come. If Mast did find himself really close-pressed, he'd merely pull back into hiding and wait. Wait with infinite patience until, finally, everyone gave up and that threat was past. Then he'd emerge from hiding and resume his private war.

The *only* way to get Mast, it seemed to Parry, would be to draw him in close somehow. Bait a trap and catch him in it. They'd all discussed as much at some length. But how in hell could it be done? Nobody had any idea.

Right now guards were laid up in hiding outside Alder Kane's house, and Mast could supposedly be nailed if he made any kind of approach to the place. Parry had bleak doubts on that score. So far Mast hadn't made any try in that direction. He might even know about the guards (he seemed to know everything else) and was waiting in the patient and canny knowledge that finally they would grow slack.

Or else he had something entirely different in his skewed mind.

Parry shook his head wearily. There was just no way of outguessing the bastard. None he could think of, and for days he'd raked over every possibility till he was sick with thinking. His nerves were worn raw, his temper so close to a hairtrigger that he was constantly bracing to hold in.

They came onto a rise north of headquarters and saw the buildings. On their left, indigo light was peeling out of the sky, chasing the last gold and crimson strata of sunset. The ranch layout was washed in a mellow light and all was peaceful.

Wordlessly they rode on and, by tacit consent, swung wide of the fir groves that flanked the outsheds and corrals, keeping clear of the buildings, too. Parry was waiting for Soholt or Genardo to sing out. This late in the day, both of them should be about. There should be lights in the bunkhouse, smoke of a supper fire showing.

And whereabouts was Barney? He ought to be raising a ruckus at their approach.

Parry lifted a hand for a halt, then gave everything a careful study.

What was it one lad in his company used to say—back when they were entrenched in front of Vicksburg? On almost any night when Parry would make a tour of the sentry line and ask Private Chalmers how things were out there, Chalmers would say the same thing: "Real quiet, sir," and invariably add, "Maybe too *damn* quiet, sir."

But there . . . orange squares of light were forming in the two bunkhouse windows. A lamp had been lighted. And smoke was just starting to puff from the roofstack. With the Parrys gone, the two hands would be preparing a solitary supper on the bunkroom stove.

Still Parry hesitated. After a moment he lifted his voice in a shout:

"Bill! Genardo!"

At once Barney's muffled barking, eager and joyous, came from the bunkhouse.

Linc chuckled. His weather-dark and usually stoical face betrayed a faint break of relief. "Old Barn's doin' fine. I reckon they brought him in there for company. I ought to take him out for a run."

Parry nodded. "Do that. I'll have a look in the house."

Linc swung his mount toward the bunkhouse. Parry rode on to the main house and stepped down, looped his rein around the hitchrail, and tramped up on the veranda. He slipped the doorlatch and, before nudging open the door with his foot, drew his Colt. These days it was instinct with him to slip out his gun before he entered any unoccupied room, or a woodshed or stable or even an outhouse, because he could never be sure what was just beyond the door.

Parry stepped into the front parlor and moved slowly through the house. The rooms were dim with nearing twilight, but he could make everything out clear enough. He prowled through all the downstairs rooms and then went upstairs.

As he reached the top landing, a whiff of something pungent and foul, like rotting meat, hit his nostrils. His shoulder muscles bunched; tension clenched in his chest. He paused for a long moment, listening. And moved slowly forward, the Colt up and ready.

Then he came to a stop. The door of Ariel's room was open. He sidled up to the doorway, braced for anything. An odd humming filled the room and now the stench was overpowering.

On the bed, neatly centering the mattress that had been stripped of its blankets, was the carcass of a skinned chicken. Half-rotted and stinking, spreading a stain of dark wet foulness around it . . . what he could see of it through the buzzing swarm of flies.

Sweet Jesus!

Parry wheeled and pounded down the stairs and out the door. He halted on the veranda, his blood congealing as he looked toward the bunkhouse.

The two small high windows no longer showed light. They were like squared eyes, dark and enigmatic. No sound at all. Linc's horse stood by the closed door, reins thrown. But Linc was nowhere in sight.

Parry opened his mouth to call out. And then didn't. A dozen terrified impulses raged at once in his brain; an iron caution flagged down each one.

If he crossed the open compound to reach the bunkhouse, he'd be in clear view all the way. Parry turned back into the house, crossed to its far side, punched out the square of oiled paper in a window, and climbed out across the sill. Cut off from the bunkhouse now, he made a broad circle through the stands of fir trees, keeping them always between him and any vantage from the bunkhouse.

No windows on its north side. He moved up close beside it, hugging the thick log walls, pausing to set an ear against a crack in the clay chinking. He couldn't detect the faintest noise. Not even a growl out of Barney.

Parry sidled along to the far corner, turned it and moved at a half-crouch along the west side, edged around the front corner, and was right up by the door now.

Parry's body was crawling with sweat. His mouth was dry as a kiln, his belly tight and hard, filled with the sick pulse of his blood.

Go right in and you'll walk into something sure. But what choice did he have? Linc was in there . . . and so was Mast. *For damned sure.*

As was customary with many high-country bunkhouses, the single door opened into a small gloomy tackroom you had to pass through to reach the bunk area. The tackroom was heaped with old trunks, boxes, heterogeneous gear on each side, a narrow aisle running between. It was windowless; the only two windows in the whole building were in the bunkroom, south-facing to catch the sunlight.

Go in fast. Don't think about it.

Parry pressed the Colt against his side to muffle the sound as he cocked it. Very gently, using the hook on his right wrist, he noiselessly raised the loose-set latch. Then he kicked the door open and lunged suddenly inside, pivoting on his heel with his Colt ready.

Quick as his move was, it wasn't quick enough. The near darkness of the tackroom briefly confused him. In that instant something snaked out of the shadows and snapped over his extended gun arm.

It was, he fleetingly realized, a gleaming strand of wire with a snare loop at the end. Yanking over his wrist, it sawed deep into his flesh. He yelled out with the searing pain and jerked the Colt's trigger in reflex. The shot thundered offside into a wall. Something on the other end of the wire, a hulking shadow of a shape, gave it a mighty heaving pull.

The sheer animal power of it swung Parry around in a helpless arc, backpedaling. He tripped and crashed on his back amid a clutter of gear. Quick as thought the dark shape was looming above him, arm raised, its fist chopping down.

Whatever the fist held crashed against his skull and sent him pinwheeling into darkness. . . .

CHAPTER TWELVE

Parry wasn't completely unconscious, just badly stunned.

But he was near helpless, splotches of light and dark swimming in his vision, as he felt hands grab him by the ankles and drag him from the storage area into the darkened bunkroom. He was also aware of being rolled on his belly, his arms yanked behind him, and another agonizing bite of wire as the noose on his left hand was locked fast to the stump of his other arm.

Gasping raggedly, his face turned sideways on the splintery floor, he heard a match being struck. His eyes were starting to clear as the lamp was lighted, spreading a raw glow through the room. The wolflike face of Josey Mast materialized out of the dimness.

Mast said lazily, "Hey there, Cap'n, how's it hangin'," as he set the lamp on the trestle table toward the east end of the room.

It was amazing how little the man had changed in all these years.

Even the hardships of prison life had hardly altered Mast's appearance. He was as gaunt as a famished wolf, yet so tall and huge-boned that he seemed massive, towering in the sallow light. His head was lean and hawklike, with a great hooked beak of a nose. No trace of prison pallor showed on his nut-brown face. His stringy black hair and beard framed it with a dark malevolence, though neither had grown out much in the weeks since his escape.

The eyes were particularly strange. Cavernous and deepsunk, brightly pale and unblinking, startling in his dark face. They were full of a cold intelligence that seemed more animal than human. Parry remembered Mast's eyes best of all. Holding his straight-on gaze had always made him uneasy.

His clothing was ragged and faded and nondescript, likely pieced together from several stolen garments, for it surely wasn't a prison outfit. He wore tall moccasins that were folded down at the knees.

Gritting his teeth, Parry managed with a mighty effort to roll onto his back. It gave him a better vantage. The lamplight washed the log walls fitfully, reaching only dimly to the corners of the room. He saw Linc sprawled on a bunk, head back and mouth open. His eyes were closed, his feet bound, his hands tied in front of him.

"What . . . did you do . . . to him?" Parry's voice echoed in the splitting pain of his own head.

Mast slung a hip onto a corner of the table, half-sitting, negligently toying with a revolver. He raised it to eye level, pointed it at Linc's head, squinted along the sights, and murmured, "Ping." Then he lowered the revolver and looked back at Parry, his long jaw dropping in a vast grin that showed his yellowish canine teeth.

"Why shoot, Cap'n, not a thing, 'cept I tapped him with this here"—he motioned with the gun barrel—"like I done you, when he come barging in. That is a right peart boy, but he's like his pappy one way. Gets careless betimes."

Parry blinked and tried to shake the fog out of his head, his glance touching now on Barney. The big hound lay on his side against a wall, legs trussed together, a rawhide cord tied around his snout. He whimpered softly through his locked jaws.

Mast chuckled, lounged to his feet, and walked over to the dog. "Mighty peart hound, too. But Cap'n, I'm half critter myself. Fancy critters a hell of a lot better'n any human bein' I ever met. They know it, too. Brung along a few meat scraps to give your pooch and he quieted right down. Figured, though, he mought get a mite upset if he seen me clout you fellers, so I cinched him up for a spell."

Mast hunkered down and scratched Barney behind the ears, and his deep, gravelly voice softened. "Hey, pooch. You be fine as maidenhair now, uh? Sure you will. Here . . ."

Mast pulled a Bowie knife and cut the rawhide thongs. Barney rolled to his feet, shook himself, and then sat down facing Mast, tongue lolling and tail wagging. Parry couldn't quite believe what he was seeing.

"That's how she is, Cap'n. Allus been that way. Critters is my kind. Ain't hardly killed a one cep'n to eat. Well . . . that horse o' yourn, I done that for sure. Too bad. And them chickens o' yourn, I surely wrung their necks. But I needed to spook you, and shit, I never fancied chickens all that much."

Chuckling, Mast rubbed Barney's head and then got to his feet.

"Like that dumb little hoor in town, too. You know 'bout that? Sure you do. Had naught agin her long as she behaved right. She's my sort, likewise. None of your prissy-tailed respectables. By grab, I really shined to that little hoor."

"My men," Parry husked between his teeth. "What did you do with my men?"

"Oh, them."

Mast resettled his butt on the corner of the table and thumb-nudged his battered slouch hat to the back of his head. His tattered clothing was ingrained with filth and even from a couple yards away his unwashed odor of old sweat and bodily wastes was rank in Parry's nostrils.

"They wa'n't no odds atall, Cap'n. After I shook you gents off awhile back, I seen you and your boy was heading for here. So I hustled to get ahead o' you. The old Mex was here alone and I jus' grabbed him an' trussed him up like a hog. The other guy come in off-range just after and I laid for him by the stable and coldcocked him jus' as easy. Left 'em both back in the woodshed yonder, all tied up 'n' gagged so's they be out o' the way. Got nothin' agin 'em, but didn't want 'em raisin' a ruction whilst I laid for you."

Mast let out another gravelly chuckle. "Thing is, Cap'n, I got naught agin anyone savin' them as done me dirt. Mostly, that's you. But they was others. Like Judge Venner. I nailed him cold—you know that? Well, I did, right inside his own house in Galena. Yeh boy, that ol' prison grapevine is somethin'. Man can keep track of jus' about anything happens on the outside, he wants to bad enough and iffen he knows the system. And I done it. Man, I done it all them years. I follered what every damn one of you bastids was doin' all that time."

Mast shifted his hip on the table. He broke the loading gate of his revolver, spilled the cartridges into his palm, and peered into the chambers. He began to reload, punching each shell into place with brief, savage jabs. The toothy, baleful smile held on his lips.

"So I knowed right where to find ol' Sarge Mulhare, too. He made a career of the army till he got out of the service a couple year ago. Then he took up farmin' outside o' Dubuque, Ioway. Well, I laid up outside his house one night and when he come out next mornin' to milk his cows— ping!—I shot ol' Sarge square through the head. Never knowed what hit him."

Mast snapped the loading gate back into place.

"There was men on that jury that sentenced me I wouldn't of minded dustin' off neither. But I wa'n't that set up about them. They was small fish. Some of 'em's died by now, or they've moved elsewhere, or what-not. Didn't really make no never-mind to me." Mast paused, eyeing his revolver. He gave a slow, speculative nod. "There's jus' one man o' that bunch around Galena I'd of liked to of fetched and I couldn't. That was Constable Bart Hanson. Remember, Cap'n? Hanson was the one arrested me as what he called a 'prime suspect' for doin' in that gal Prissy Evans. Which I done for sure, if you ever wondered. But Hanson, I learned he died of nat'ral causes, back seven years ago."

Mast casually sighted the revolver at Linc's head again, said "Ping," and then looked back at Parry.

"Course there was Tom Redfern . . . good ol' Tom. I'd of admired to bag Tom's ass too, 'fore I got to you. But it wa'n't so easy to cut sign on Tom. Bounty-huntin', he's kept on the move a lot. He'll keep a spell longer. Tom is a humdinger. He won't be no easy mark and that's fine. Man gets plumb tired of pickin' off easy marks. And I got all the time in the world."

That was something, Parry thought numbly. Not much, but something. Apparently Mast wasn't aware that Tom Redfern, knowing of his escape, would be on the hunt for *him*, not the other way around. Or, if Mast had given the possibility any consideration, he wasn't much concerned about it.

Right now, Mast was in no hurry. He wanted to talk, wanted to brag it up. All right, Parry thought. Play for time. Let him talk.

"Josey," he said huskily, "I guess you have that. Lots of time, lots of patience. Man who could wait that long. Plan that hard."

"You betcha, Cap'n." Mast nodded with a kind of pleased, droll agreement. "That Joliet Prison, man, that ain't no place to break out of. I knowed plenty guys tried to bust out of stony lonesome. They allus got caught. Or got kilt tryin'. They's some tried to get me in on their breakouts. I'd allus tell 'em real polite, no. I jus' went on waitin' and behavin' myself. There was a prison farm outside that a man could get transferred to if he behaved hisself long enough. Outside the walls . . . that's where a man has gotta make his break.

"A year ago I got moved out to the farm and I went right on waitin', workin' in the fields. Man, I worked like a dog. Done it deliberate. Wanted to keep up my strength, y'know? And it sure helped git the guards less 'n' less suspicious. One day I jus' walked away from the fields. They put hounds on me, but that didn't take worth shit. Hounds, see, they're trained to foller one smell. They lose that and they're done up." Mast's shoulders shook with silent laughter. "All I done was, I got a ways from the farm and I smeared my shoes with cowshit I found in a neighborin' pasture and then kept goin'."

"That was pretty smart," Parry said.

"Yeh, well . . ." Mast gave a modest shrug. "After that I was free game in an open field, but I could make my own rules. Done pretty fair at it, I reckon."

"Look," Parry said, grimacing a little, "do you mind if I sit up?"

"Shoot no, Cap'n. Long as you can make it by yourself."

Mast watched amusedly as Parry heaved himself up till he was resting on his butt, no easy task with his arms tied. He hitched himself backward, awkwardly, till his shoulders came up against the log wall.

"Mast . . . listen. You've got me in hand, for whatever it's worth to you. Do whatever you want with me. Just leave my family out of it."

As he spoke, Parry was dully aware there'd be nothing gained by arguing with the man. Mast's pattern of persecution had been set long ago. He'd lived with it, refined it over and over in his skewed brain for years. No line of rational argument would throw him off it. For Parry, this was just another way to stall for time.

But time for *what*? It was hard to think above the battering pain that filled his head.

Mast's lip curled without easing his grin. Then he threw back his head and laughed. "Aw, Cap'n. You are a caution to snakes, for sure. Hell, why should I leave 'em out of it?"

"They never did you any harm, did they?"

Mast leaned forward a little. His eyes shone wickedly in the lampglow. "Let's say it all pleasures me, Cap'n. I'm getting a heap o' fun out of this. Shit, I coulda taken you out any time I wanted. I took a bead on you over my rifle sights a few times you mighta guessed about, plenty more times you never knowed about. But it woulda been too easy. Too goddam quick. Cap'n, when I get to dustin' you off, it ain't gonna come easy or quick."

Now Mast settled back with a contented chuckle. "Specially since there's that purty little red-haired gal o' yourn. I'm gonna get to her 'fore I get to you. And you're gonna know all about it when I do."

Parry closed his jaws so tightly that they ached. Finally he said shakily, "All right. Only answer me this. Why? I never gave you any offense you didn't ask for. Back in the war I went out of my way to take your part whenever you landed yourself in trouble."

Mast gave a small, comfortable nod. "Cap'n, you done that. You surely did."

"Then why? Why lay all this on me?"

"I tell you why." Mast's tone turned ice-cold, full of a pure hate. "Because headin' our outfit, you always carried yourself so goddam high and fancy. You had a proper way of sayin' and doin' everything like you was born to it. Only you wasn't."

God, Parry thought, was that it? Had something as slight

as that made him the prime focus of whatever had festered in Mast's primitive mind all this time?

"No," he said slowly. "I wasn't. All I did was pull myself up by my bootstraps. In this country any man's free to do the same. And nobody did it for me."

"Yeah," Mast said softly. "That's it, Cap'n. I know all 'bout you. You was nothin' but the son of a mick stablehand before you come west to Pisstown, Illinois, with your highsteppin' Boston lady. Then you become cock of the walk all at once. Cozied yourself up next to Sam Grant. You was too goddam good for all us lowdown tackies in the ranks."

"Mast, it wasn't like that. I never felt that way—"

"Shet your goddam mouth," Mast said casually. "Christ, I hate all you eddicated-up-to-the-eyes bastids. I allus did. But man, you are the fine-haired livin' prize of the lot."

A soft moan came from Linc. He was stirring on the bunk, starting to revive. Mast's glance shifted to him, and with Mast's attention averted, Parry gave a strong wrench at the wire that secured his wrists.

A red agony shot up through his arms. He felt warm trickles of blood on his hand and stump from the deep bite of wire. But on his right forearm, he thought the wire slipped a little. It was looped over the wristbone end of the handless arm, from which Mast had already stripped the leather-jacket hook.

A few more strong yanks and maybe he could free his arms. Parry gave another hard wrench, and then Mast's glance shuttled back to him.

"Your boy is comin' to, Cap'n. That's fine. What I want is, I want him to know jus' what I'm gonna do. But it won't be worth a damn if you ain't watchin' me do it."

Parry didn't reply.

Mast eased to his feet, his face gaunt and sallow. "What I gonna do is, I'm gonna chop his hand off. So's it'll be like yours, only on his other arm, see, the *left* one. It will kind o' balance you fellers out, then. Like father, like son, I allus say."

Jesus God.

Momentarily, Parry's brain froze. But now he had a goal in mind—to slip his hand free—and he could manage to reply slowly and deliberately. *Anything to stall a little longer!*

"Mast, you're crazy. Do you know that? You're as crazy as a bedbug."

Mast tipped his head mockingly, almost genially. "Yeh. I been told that before. Even when I was a kid, they was folks told me so. Thing is, I never looked at it that way. I allus allowed I was jus' born mean. Maybe you can't feature somethin' like that, Cap'n. But there's guys born that way. I met a right smart of 'em when I was in the pen. Yep. Some of us, we's jus' born plain fuckin' mean."

My God, Parry thought.

Mast gave his grating chuckle and pulled his Bowie knife as he moved over to the bunk. Parry tensed his muscles to give one mighty tug that might—or might not—free his arms.

Barney let out a mild, querulous whine. Mast halted, the blade poised in his hand. He looked at the hound and his gaze softened.

"Hell, pooch," he said gently. "You gonna get your hackles up about it? I reckon you will, at that. Don't blame you none. We'll jus' put you out o' sight while it's doin'."

Mast crossed to the storeroom door, motioning to Barney. Wagging his tail, Barney followed him into the storeroom.

At once Parry jerked savagely at his bound wrists, twisting them in opposite directions. He felt the wire give a little more, slick with blood as it pulled lower, tearing flesh.

Mast stepped back into the bunkroom, closing the door

behind him. Barney woofed and scratched behind it. Mast grinned at Parry and walked back to the bunk where Linc was coming fully awake, groggy and groaning.

Mast bent above him. "Boy," he murmured, "so far you ain't got a lot to make much noise about. But you will now, by Jesus. . . ."

He set the knife and cut, a sudden and savage sweep of the blade.

Linc screamed.

Parry gave another savage, tearing pull at the wire. He felt his right arm jerk free.

He rolled up on his haunches, then sprang to his feet and leaped sidelong at Mast.

CHAPTER THIRTEEN

Quick as thought Mast spun around to face him, the bloody knife up and ready. Even in the red rage that gripped him, Parry had the presence of mind to haul up short. In an instant Mast had reversed the knife in his palm so that the cutting edge was turned upward. Lamplight dribbled along the razor-honed blade.

Not at all disconcerted, Mast nodded gently. "That's smart, Cap'n. One more step and I'll split you clean up the middle. Lay you open as neat as I'd gut a channel cat."

The two men were faced off against each other a couple yards apart, Mast sunk to a graceful crouch, like a great angular puma.

Parry was swaying unsteadily on his feet. Mast's soft words cut clean and clear through Linc's groans and Barney's frenzied barking. Parry knew that Mast was likely as strong as him, had a longer reach, and was a lot faster for sure, quick as lightning. His own gun and Mast's rifle lay on the table a few feet away, but if he made a grab for either, Mast would be on him in an instant.

Linc was writhing on the bunk, his wrists still bound, blood spurting from one.

"You want it now," Mast said in a taunting drone, "you come right ahead, Cap'n. I'll rip your tripe out quicker'n a cooncat can shinny up a hick'ry tree. I can still do

ever'thing else like I planned. Course you won't be around
to know 'bout it and I'll be right sorry 'bout that. . . ."

Mast's voice trailed. His gaze flicked past Parry to the
nearest of the two small windows.

Unexpectedly, without a word, he hunched his shoulders
and barreled straight at Parry. His left shoulder smashed into
Parry's right shoulder, knocked him aside and sent him
floundering backward. Off balance, Parry managed to keep
on his feet, and Mast was lunging past him for the storeroom door.

He wrenched it open just as the window shattered, a
shower of glass bursting inward. The thunder of a gunshot
filled the room.

Then Mast was going out through the door, unhit,
springing across the storeroom toward the outside door.
Barney's wild yapping drowned every other sound for a
moment. More gunshots then, and an angry roar from Mast.

Parry stumbled out through the storeroom, grabbing at
the frame of the outside door for support. Mast had already
commandeered Linc's horse, and now he was racing away
in the twilight, bent low and tight to the animal's mane.

The gun spoke once more, and then the hammer hit an
empty chamber, followed by a man's low curse.

Mast was going away fast, and soon he was lost to sight
around a clump of fir trees.

Parry stood gripping the doorframe, his mouth open,
gasping shallowly. His belly was boiling with tension that
was only half-released. Now a man came striding around
the corner of the bunkhouse and hauled up, facing him.

It was Tom Redfern.

"You all right, Cap'n?" he asked.

"Yes . . . my boy . . . he . . ."

"I know. I saw some of it. Let's get in there and fix him
up."

Redfern holstered his Colt .45 and brushed past Parry,

going inside. Parry followed him stumblingly. When he reached the bunkroom, Redfern already had a clasp knife out and was cutting Linc free of the cords.

"There you go, boy," he said. "No, don't sit up . . . you just lay back. No need to get pumping out more blood than you need to. I'm an old friend of your pa's. Redfern's the name. Here, let's have a look at that. . . ."

Linc was still glassy-eyed with shock and he said nothing, just did as he was told, lying back with only his head lifted. He stared at his blood-pumping wrist with a kind of numb fascination. His clothes and the bunk's rumpled blankets and straw-stuffed tick were soaked with blood.

Barney was still yapping. Parry yelled at him to shut up. The big hound came slinking into the bunkroom, sank to the floor on his belly, and rested his head on his paws, gazing at them with a melancholy reproach.

Redfern glanced at Parry. "Cap'n, we better get this cauterized fast. It's a mighty deep cut. You stoke up a fire"—he nodded toward the potbelly stove set on a stone platform at the center of the room—"and get her going good. Meantime I'll rig a tourniquet."

Like his son, Parry numbly did as he was told.

It was an almighty bad cut.

Mast's one slash had laid Linc's wrist open to the bone. With Linc's arms tied in front of him and the backs of his hands uppermost, the blood vessels on the underside of his left wrist had escaped injury. But the wound was still serious enough to need instant cautery, not just a plastering with flour (as a lot of people mistakenly did to seal hard-bleeding cuts, though it could result in serious complications). Ideally, the slash should be stitched up, but the surging gush of blood made this next to impossible.

Touch-on-touch cautery of a wound was a tricky busi-

ness. It took a sure and knowing and steady hand. But that
was an old story for Tom Redfern.

Parry's own hand was shaking badly. But it didn't impede
his quick stoking of the stove with kindling wood to get a
fire going. Meantime Redfern cinched a leather-belt tourniquet on Linc's arm, carefully tightening and loosening it at
intervals.

As the woodfire began a drafty roar up the stovestack,
Parry gave Redfern a dazed glance. "Jesus," he said. "I
forgot. The two men on my crew . . . he said he left 'em
tied up in the woodshed."

Redfern nodded. "Go get 'em free. They'll be a help. I'll
tend your boy." He added gently, "Take it easy, Cap'n. Just
swallow wind a few times, real deep, and take a hold on
yourself."

Good advice.

Parry had been out of law work too many years. The
strain on his nerves these last days had been terrific, and
what had just happened had left him so rattled it was hard to
think.

In five minutes he'd freed Bill Soholt and Genardo
Menocal, and they were all back at the bunkhouse. Calmly
and sensibly, Tom Redfern suggested that one of them take
up a watch outside, in case Mast should circle back. Going
out of there lickety-split, like he had, it wasn't likely he'd
be back right away. For once *he'd* been the one caught off
guard. But it wouldn't hurt to keep a lookout. Genardo said
he'd take the watch.

With a good bed of coals glowing in the potbelly stove, a
knifeblade was thrust in and heated red-hot.

All they had for anesthetic was whiskey. Linc managed to
swallow a few generous slugs from the bottle that Soholt
produced, but his stomach rebelled almost at once and he
threw up most of it. For once Parry regretted his son's

distaste for liquor. He and Soholt pinioned Linc's arms and legs while Redfern did the job.

It wasn't just a tricky piece of business; it was a nasty and nightmarish one. His son's screams and the stench of seared flesh made Parry come close to throwing up, too. Luckily, Linc passed out after the first few touches of the superheated blade, and then Redfern completed the cautery quickly and expertly. . . .

When it was over, Parry and Redfern and Soholt passed the whiskey bottle around, each of them downing a stiff jolt. They needed it. Linc was still unconscious, and he might remain so for quite a spell, Redfern said.

By now the twilight had faded into early darkness. All of them had missed supper, but nobody felt like eating. Soholt said that he'd join Genardo on watch outside. He felt too damn squirrelly to do anything else.

Will Parry and Tom Redfern sat at the bunkroom table and talked. After sixteen years, they had a great deal of things to discuss, even aside from the immediate trouble. They brewed up a big pot of coffee on the potbelly stove and they drank cup after cup as they talked.

Parry told Redfern what Mast had told him about how he'd escaped Joliet Prison. Redfern, in turn, explained why he hadn't arrived in Chinook Basin as soon as he'd hoped. A killer that Redfern had tracked and captured had escaped just after Redfern had delivered the fellow to the sheriff at Trinidad, Colorado, where a warrant had been sworn out for his arrest, along with the offer of a large reward.

Just after he'd brought in his prisoner, Redfern had first learned of Josey Mast's escape from Joliet and of the murders of Judge Venner and Sean Mulhare. At once he'd dispatched the warning telegram to Parry in Chinook Basin. But right afterward, the killer had broken out of jail, and Redfern had felt duty-bound to aid the local sheriff in his recapture. It had taken longer than expected. So, despite the need for haste, Redfern hadn't arrived in Salvation until today.

After learning from Alder Kane about the current state of affairs, and not knowing where to look for Will Parry right away since he was out on posse, Redfern had headed for WP headquarters. A sudden hunch had told him to waste no time getting here.

Parry knew the feeling. He'd been hit by it often enough back in his days as a peace officer, and lately he'd felt it just as frequently. Most times the dark intuitions came to nothing, but a man learned not to ignore them.

Maybe that same extra sense had made Redfern cautious as he'd approached the headquarters. He hadn't noted anything particularly amiss, except that the whole layout had seemed just a bit too tranquil. There was a horse tied in front of the main house, another by the bunkhouse. Nothing suspicious that he could put his finger on. But slowly reconnoitering the place, he had come on a sorrel horse that was tethered in the fir trees north of the buildings, obviously to conceal it.

That was the tip-off.

Redfern had tied his own animal back in the trees, then had stolen carefully up on the bunkhouse. Getting close to a window, he'd caught a tense murmur of voices from within. Knowing just how dangerously alert Josey Mast could be, Redfern had hesitated to make another move until he heard Linc's sudden cry of pain. A quick look through the small window had showed him Parry, his arms freed, lunging at Mast, who had quickly rounded on him, making it a stand-off.

Because Parry was between Mast and him, Redfern couldn't at once draw a bead on Mast. Then Mast had spotted him at the window, gun leveled, and had knocked Parry aside to get past him and out the door. Redfern had broken the window to take a snap shot at Mast and missed, his bullet driving into the log wall.

After the two of them had compared experiences, Redfern said gravely, "Well, that's about it, Cap'n. Mast is out to rack up both our hides. He'll do it sure, if we don't fetch him first. You got the worst of it because you got family. He can get at you through them. Me, I'm a lonesome and footloose man. Got no living kin to speak of."

Parry nodded, staring into his coffee cup, swirling the dregs around. "And you'd be the hardest to find . . . the hardest one to run down. He liked that idea. He'd save you for the last, he said."

"Sure," Redfern said. "But he's got it in for you the most, Cap'n. Hell, he always hated your guts, even when he had no good reason. I seen that way back in the war."

Parry glanced up with a faint smile. It was the kind of wry, haunted smile that a man could summon up when he had the feeling his string was running out. Redfern smiled back.

Tom Redfern was of medium height, almost slight of build. But his slenderness was deceptive. That had been true even sixteen years ago when Redfern, a boy of eighteen or so, had proven his mettle on the toughest of wartime patrols. This older Redfern was trouble-seasoned, wiry, and he looked as tough as rawhide. His bony, narrow-jawed face was weathered and seamed, bisected by a drooping yellow mustache that half-hid his mouth. His light eyebrows were almost invisible, hooding deepset eyes that were pale and guarded. He wore an old buckskin jacket and faded blue army pants, worn and rusty, now darkly speckled with Linc's blood.

"He wants you to last, Cap'n," Redfern said gently. "He means to stretch it out for you long as he can." Maybe it was an unconscious but sharp change in Parry's expression that made him add, "I say something wrong, Cap'n?"

Parry rubbed his hand slowly over his face, blinking. A crushing tiredness dragged at his thoughts. "No. It's just . . . that's what Mast kept calling me. Cap'n."

Redfern smiled. "Well, all of us in the old outfit did. Sort of habit, you know? I can make it whatever you want. Parry? Mr. Parry?"

"Make it Will."

Redfern nodded, leaning back in his chair. "Like I said. We got to fetch him, you and me, before he fetches us. The sooner we set out, the better."

"Yeah." Parry settled both his arms on the table, looking bleakly at his hand and his hook. "That's what my boy said." He glanced at Linc, still unconscious on the bunk. "A couple men working together might be able to outflank Mast. A posse of men can't. Or even a whole passel of posses. But damn it, Tom! Linc is a woodsman and he's good. But Mast . . . he's *too* damned good. He'd have picked Linc and me off like sitting ducks. You think that just you and me . . . ?"

"No way of saying for sure," Redfern said quietly. "But I don't reckon we got any choice. Me, I'm going out after him. I'd admire to have you along, Will. You want to come?"

Not hesitating, Parry nodded. "I can call the posses off. Tell 'em to go home. I'll take my chances with you, Tom. If any man's got the know-how, it ought to be you."

"Maybe so, maybe no. We'll find out." Redfern pushed back his chair and stood up. "I better go look to the horses. We'll keep a guard on the place tonight, take the watch turnabout, along with your men. I don't reckon he'll be comin' back right away." He gestured at Mast's rifle on the table. "He had to leave that, and from what you say, he's only got a pistol and a knife now."

Parry said slowly, "He let out a roar when you shot at him outside. Could it be you hit him?"

Redfern shook his head. "I never touched him, sorry to say. He was just mad as hell. No damn way of telling just what he'll try next. But he'll have to get close up to his next target to try it. Gives us a little edge . . . unless he's got another rifle cached somewhere. Or less'n he can steal another one."

"He'll do that easily enough, if he wants," Parry said grimly. "You can count on it."

Redfern nodded. "Might take him off of us for a while, anyway."

Linc let out a soft groan.

"Your boy is coming to," Redfern said. "We can take turns tending to him. Right now, I think you better get some sleep. I'll wake you in a couple hours."

Parry covered a vast yawn with his hand, realizing just how tired he was. "All right. But God, Tom . . . he needs a doctor."

"Sure he does," Redfern agreed. "Soon as we can get him to town. But it's pitch dark out and we better wait till first light. You get some sleep now, Will."

CHAPTER FOURTEEN

LEAH PARRY WOKE SUDDENLY. SHE LAY LISTENING IN THE gray dimness. The rosy light of true dawn was still a couple hours away, but she could pick out objects in the room plainly enough.

She didn't know what, if anything, had brought her out of a deep sleep. After a couple of near-sleepless nights, her nerves keenly on edge, she'd asked Dr. Costiner for a sedative. One small packet of the powders he gave her put her straight to sleep. When the sedative wore off, she might come awake at any sound . . . or for no reason at all.

A little groggily, Leah stretched an arm to one side, wanting as usual to touch Will's warm, reassuring bulk. Then she remembered that he and Linc hadn't come back last night. One of the returning possemen had dropped by to tell her that the two of them had split off for WP headquarters to make a close-up check on things.

They must have decided to stay over at the ranch. Rather than spend a night waiting and worrying about—probably— nothing at all, she'd taken the powders as usual and had dropped off at once. Restless now, the worry rushing back sharply, she knew she would get no more sleep, and she might as well have a look at Timmy.

Swinging out of bed, Leah shivered and rubbed her arms. It was always coldest when morning was making, the light of predawn stirring the still air of night into slow, chilly currents. She toed into her slippers, threw on a thick wool wrapper over her flannel nightgown, and slipped quietly from the room.

She didn't need much light to negotiate this second-story corridor, familiar to her by now, and reassuringly similar to the sleeping area at home. The sheriff and his wife occupied a room to the right, and to the left were Tim's and Linc's and Ariel's rooms.

Leah glanced in first on Ariel. She was sleeping soundly, her red hair (darkly auburn in this light) crumpled on the pillow, a hand knuckled lightly against her cheek.

Leah smiled, a little wryly. All three kids had better nerves than Will or her. Were we like that when we were young? she wondered. Perhaps so. Hard to tell when you'd never in your life had to face anything like . . . like the present situation.

She thought of Josey Mast as something inhuman. A stark threat to the ordered world she and Will had made for themselves and the kids. Leah felt a fierce protectiveness, a determination that nothing must harm them, no danger must touch any of them again.

But it was merely a feeling, she knew. No kind of assurance at all.

Next she looked in on Tim. He was snoring lightly and evenly in the good sleep of healing. He was coming along fine, Dr. Costiner had declared with satisfaction.

For Leah there would be no more rest tonight, but that was all right. Lately she'd fallen into a ritual of getting up as soon as she woke and going downstairs to lay a fire, get breakfast under way.

She tiptoed down to the kitchen, lighted a lamp on the table and then, moving as quietly as she could, got a fire going in the big range. Kate Kane and she were lucky to be provided with comforts that a lot of town and ranch wives in this remote Wyoming basin didn't have. Many of them still cooked on potbelly stoves or in fireplaces equipped with trammels and pothooks from which kettles could be hung . . . or where skillets could be set on live coals that might crumble and dump a whole meal into the ashes.

Leah filled the coffeepot with water, added Triple X ground coffee, and set the pot on a stovelid. Then she went over to a window and gazed out at the gray false dawn that was rimming the horizon, showing the black outlines of the town buildings. The Kane house was on an isolated lot, and that had made her uneasy from the day the Parrys had moved in.

On the other hand, that slight isolation gave the two men posted on watch a better vantage of the place than they could have commanded otherwise. One guard was stationed alongside the stable in back of the house. The other was laid up beside a small cabin across the street, owned by a crabbed old bachelor named Henry Buttrick, and Buttrick himself took an occasional turn at guard duty. Shrubbery beside the buildings gave both guards a good cover, and their positions were angled so that each had a clear view of two sides of the Kane house. Anyone approaching it, no matter which way he came, would be picked up. Inside, Alder Kane kept a shotgun close to hand at all times; his wife Kate was handy with both pistol and rifle.

Leah hated guns.

Even as a child she'd taken an early abhorrence to them after seeing her father and three brothers, all ardent sportsmen, come in from a day's hunt laden with the bloodied carcasses of rabbit and quail. And proficiency with firearms had never been an art grilled into a young lady of decorous accomplishments back in staid and settled Boston. Still, she'd lived with a mildly guilty awareness that her personal aversion to guns had had as much to do with her husband's decision to give up a lawman's career as did the allure of this Wyoming basin. Or the wartime amputation of his hand.

Out here, realistically, it was an unfortunate aversion for any woman to have. Even in well-settled country, men liked to hunt and took pride in their ability with guns. Having followed her own man west, she was supposed to accept stolidly the lot of any ranch wife. In most ways she'd done so. And Will had made his own concessions to her feelings, more than most men would. But underneath it all, Leah didn't feel any differently. She'd always felt a silent revulsion toward Linc's passion for hunting, even though it kept their table supplied with fresh meat. . . .

A floorboard creaked behind Leah. She whirled around. Kate stood in the kitchen doorway, a gray wrapper around her ample form, and she yawned and smiled.

"Didn't mean to startle you, dearie. But I couldn't sleep any more either. Saints alive, but it's gettin' to be a fray on the nerves, isn't it?"

Leah smiled back and folded her arms, massaging them with her fingertips. "It is. But I wish you and Mr. Kane hadn't gotten mixed into our troubles."

"Now, now, we've been over all that," Kate said cheerfully. "I dealt myself into a lifelong peck o' worry when I married a man who's in law work. That's the way of things. You're grand folks, you and your mister and the kids, and it's a pleasure havin' you about. I had five brothers and five sisters, and I've borne me a raft of kids, and I can tell you, dearie, this livin' in a big empty house has been no way to my taste." She nodded at the coffeepot, now coming to a good boil on the stove. "Right now I could stand a mean cup of java. Trust you've made it strong enough to float a horseshoe nail?"

"Of course. Don't I always?"

"Well . . ." Kate crossed to a cupboard and took out two tin cups, then went over to the stove and sniffed at the bubbling brew. "Oh my, yes. You're a Western wife for sure, Lee."

Leah laughed. Kate's brisk good humor was a Godsend, always giving a lift to her spirits. Living way out in the Basin, she'd often missed the woman talk that she could enjoy only on shopping trips in town, or at occasional church socials or barn-raisings or the like.

She said, "Why don't we go out to the chicken house, Kate? See if your hens have got up some fresh eggs for breakfast."

"Plenty o' time before we got to be laying out breakfast for the troops." Kate wrapped a rag around her hand and grasped the coffeepot handle. She began to fill the cups. "Let's be sittin' down a bit for some coffee and chatter. Then—"

The latch on the back door rattled softly.

Kate broke off in mid-speech and froze in place, coffeepot in hand. Both women stared at the door.

No other sound followed. The latch didn't stir again.

But both of them had the same instant thought. Neither of the outside guards would try to open the door in a cautious way. They would knock first. What anyone trying to gain a stealthy entrance wouldn't know was that the latch was padlocked on the inside—a precaution that had been taken since the Parrys had moved in.

Kate shot a warning glance at Leah. Then she nodded toward the rifle leaning in a far corner, loaded and ready. It was only a couple yards from where Leah stood. And she hadn't yet confessed to Kate how she felt about guns—or that she had only the barest idea of how to use one.

But Leah had only a fleeting moment to consider the matter.

There was a splintering crash as a boot drove savagely against the door. It swung inward, the latch torn from its mooring.

Josey Mast loomed on the threshold. He was huge and wild-looking, a gaunt and toothy grin parting his bearded jaws. Leah had attended the long-ago trial that had sent Mast to prison. . . . She knew him at once.

He stepped into the room, glanced at each woman, and then started toward Leah.

Kate didn't hesitate. She swung her arm back and forward, and let go of the coffeepot, hurling it at Mast's head.

The bottom edge of the heavy pot caught Mast in the temple—and the boiling contents splashed over his head. He staggered off balance and let out a wolflike howl, clapping both hands to his face.

Kate sprang forward now, running for the rifle.

But Mast's recovery was ferret-fast. Kate was less than an arm's length away as she darted past him. One hand dropped from his face and shot out and grabbed her shoulder, whirling her to a halt. His other hand slammed her a fierce clout on the jaw, knocking her to the floor.

Leah was still paralyzed by one glimpse of Mast's red and scalded face, his bared teeth a white splash in a twisted mask of pain. Now he bent and seized Kate by the throat and yanked her half-upright. He smashed a fist into her face, drew the fist back and smashed it down again.

The frozen block of terror around Leah's brain cracked. Kate's choked-off scream did it.

In the same instant something Will had told her a few days ago flashed across her mind: *All right, you can't handle a gun. But almost anything can be a weapon, Lee. Anything that's ready to hand and you can lay your hands on fast. Remember that if—*

Kate had just proven it.

Leah's glance lighted on the pile of sawed-up kindling stacked in the woodbox by the stove. She ran to it and snatched up a thick butt of kindling wood and wheeled around. It took two long steps to reach Mast, whose back was toward her.

Mast gave a feral grunt as he smashed his fist into Kate's face one more time and then let go of her, watching her slump to the floor.

A contemptuous snarl was on his lips as he began to turn. He came around just in time to catch a full-arm smash of stove-wood in his face.

Leah had hefted the piece of wood in both hands. She'd struck out blindly. The edge of the billet crushed the bridge of Mast's nose. Blood spurted. He let out a helpless roar as he floundered backward, tripped over Kate's prone form, and crashed to the floor on his back.

Leah stood swaying on her feet, immobilized by terror again. She watched Mast roll onto his side, brace a hand against the floor and start to push himself up.

She half turned toward the outside door, splintered and hanging open. *Get out of here . . . fetch help.* Then she realized in her dazed fright that no help could be brought in time.

The guards? Mast had been aware of their presence. And had managed, somehow, to put them out of commission. *Both?* Yes. He might have broken in here by taking out just one. But the noise would have brought the other man on the run.

The whole town was still abed . . . and her children were upstairs. *He'll go straight after them.*

Each icy realization chased through Leah's mind in a split-instant, even as she watched Mast roll onto his hands and knees, doggedly shaking his head.

Thought of her children sent a surge of panicked energy through her muscles. Leah took a step forward, again raising the billet two-handed to bring it down on Mast's head.

She swung with all her strength.

But she hadn't seized the advantage quickly enough. Her hesitation had given Mast the vital space of time he needed to rally a little. Suddenly his head lifted; one powerful hand shot up in the same lightning motion. The billet smacked into his spread palm. His hand closed on it. An effortless yank wrenched it from her hand and flung it aside.

Leah stumbled back as the big man heaved himself up, got one foot under him, and dragged himself upright. His face was terrible to see. It was a mask of blood that bubbled in the wreck of his shattered nose. His pale eyes were still muddy with pain and shock. But they were fixed straight on her and his mouth snarled like an animal's.

Terrified as she was, Leah could think again. Her brain went cold as ice now. The children. That resurging thought was all she needed to galvanize her into more action.

She rushed to the woodbox, seized up another piece of wood, hurled it at his face. Mast threw up an arm and batted it down in mid-flight, knocking it clattering to the floor.

He lurched toward her, his great hands outspread, his dazed look fading into a dark expression of intent and cruel fury.

He was still wobbly on his legs. It gave Leah time to dodge aside, swerving around the kitchen table. As she did, Mast was shambling around the other side to head her off.

Later on, Leah would remember how coolly her mind functioned—beyond the urge of blind instinct—in that crucial moment. Seeing that Mast would overtake her at the table's far edge, she caught hold of a chair. Jerking it away from the table, she overturned it in his path, then leaped to one side.

Mast, blundering forward and making a grab for her, couldn't stop in time. The chair tripped him up and he fell headlong. Almost at once he was scrambling up, spewing curses.

But Leah was already out of the kitchen, running through the front parlor, going up the stairs two steps at a time.

Ariel, roused by all the racket, was out of her room, coming quickly toward Leah as she reached the head of the stairs. Ariel's eyes were alight with terror.

"Ma, *what*—"

Leah was vaguely aware of Alder Kane calling from inside his room—"What is it? Kate? What's going on?"—his voice fuzzed at the edges, the confused and querulous question of a half-debilitated old man roused from sleep.

No help from that quarter. And no sound out of Tim . . . yet.

Mast's feet made thunder on the staircase as he lunged up it. Still wobbly and lurching, but coming fast.

Without a word Leah grabbed her daughter's arm and pulled her to the open door of the bedchamber that she and Will shared. She shoved Ariel in ahead of her and slammed the door shut behind them.

The room had no lock, no night bar on the door. But there was a two-barreled shotgun laid across the commode close to the bed. Will had taken the precaution of placing it there on the night they moved in.

Leah seized up the weapon. She pulled each hammer back to full cock with her thumb.

Remember this if there's any need—Will's voice echoed in her memory—*this is a Greener shotgun and the barrels are sawed off short. Get it pointed the right way, cock the hammers and pull the triggers. That's all you'll have to do, Lee. The shells are Double-Aught Buck and the shot'll have a spread so wide you can't fail to*—

Ariel stared wildly at her mother. Then her head swiveled toward the door as the heavy thump of Mast's moccasined feet paused in the corridor outside.

"Get out of the way!" Leah screamed at her.

She didn't know how much "spread" the buckshot might

have at close quarters, even if Ariel was already well to the left of her. But Ariel flinched back a few steps as Leah braced the shotgun to her shoulder.

Mast opened the door with a fierce suddenness that sent it rocking back with a crash against the wall.

His pale eyes registered the situation with an unbelievable swiftness. Quick as thought he flung himself sideways, melting to the floor as Leah jerked both triggers. The explosion of shotpowder filled the room with a shuddering, deafening roar.

Mast came bounding pantherishly to his feet, unhit.

Leah had bare moments to realize that he was already on her, the snarling face inches away as he balled the front of her nightgown in one fist, hauling her up on her toes.

The other fist drew back. It slammed her jaw like a club. And her senses spun away into blackness.

CHAPTER FIFTEEN

Sleep came hard for Will Parry that night. He kept rousing out to have a look at his son. No fever yet, but Linc slept fitfully because of the pain in his cut arm. Tom Redfern, toughened by more than one vigil of this sort, took his turn on watch and then caught a few hours rest. When false dawn began to gray the horizon, Tom was as calm and fresh as ever, ready to go. Parry's nerves were strung out, his mood irascible. But his powerful constitution wasn't easily put down. He was ready, too.

Now, with enough light to work by, the two men lost no time hacking down several slim fir trees and rigging a travois-drag made of two long poles and three cross poles and a thick bed of blankets. They tied Linc onto the litter and fastened it behind a horse.

Both Soholt and Genardo were angry and chagrined at having been so easily taken by Mast. It hadn't dampened their determination to defend the place, both men vowing they wouldn't be caught off guard again. Parry didn't argue with their matter-of-fact loyalty, but he flatly ordered that both were to restrict themselves to headquarters from now on. One was to keep a strict watch while the other slept or went about the chores. Nothing was worth any further risk to their lives. If either of them changed his mind and wanted to pull out, he ought to feel free to do so.

Bill Soholt smiled in his whimsical way. "All right, Will.

You said it. Now get that boy of yours to town. I only wish I was joining you and Mr. Redfern on the hunt."

"*Sí*," said Genardo Menocal. "It is the same with this old one."

Almost formally, Parry shook hands with each man. You couldn't buy an allegiance like theirs with all the workaday wages of a lifetime. Best to say nothing. Just shake hands with them and let it go at that. . . .

He and Tom Redfern rode out slowly, leading the litter-drag horse with Linc. The gray light turned to pearl and then reddish pink and finally to a blazing fan of yellow as the sun came up at their backs. At early morning they rode into Salvation and went directly to Dr. Costiner's house. Located at the south end of town, just across the bridge that spanned the Blackbow, it was a crude log structure that was a doctor's office and bachelor's quarters in one.

Here they learned from the tired and haggard-eyed Costiner, who'd been up all night tending to sick or injured people, what had happened just a few hours earlier.

Josey Mast must have headed straight for town and Alder Kane's home after his flight from WP headquarters. There, he wreaked much destruction. Kate Kane was now sleeping under opiates. Her jaw was broken and Costiner had just finished the lengthy and difficult job of wiring it up so the bones would knit properly.

Nils Nansen, one of the two men on guard, had a probable concussion. He hadn't yet regained consciousness. The other guard, Wilsie, was dead.

Leah was lightly drugged with opiates. Not because she was seriously injured, for she had only been knocked out cold for a brief time. But the whole experience had left her in partial shock and she'd been on the edge of hysterical grief.

Ariel was gone. Josey Mast had carried her off.

* * *

It only took Dr. Costiner a few moments to tell what had happened, as nearly as he could sort everything out.

About four o'clock that morning, Josey Mast had broken into the Alder Kane home. He'd managed it by overcoming the two men then on guard, Nils Nansen and Wilsie Manlow. That they were laid up in good cover hadn't proven any deterrent to Mast. Quite possibly he had reconnoitered the guards' positions days before. In any case—he had stolen up behind Wilsie and looped some kind of garotte over his head and strangled him to death. Likely it had been a wire rather than a cord, for Wilsie's neck had been deeply cut by its sawing pressure.

Either before that, or afterward, Mast had come up behind Nils and laid him out cold with a blow from some hard object.

Mast had broken into Kane's house through the back door and subdued both Leah and the sheriff's wife, though both had put up a hell of a resistance. Alder Kane, in sorry condition himself, hadn't been able to prevent Mast from grabbing up Ariel and escaping from the house. They were far gone by the time that a few townspeople, roused out of sleep by the sound of shotgun fire, had come on the run.

After examining Linc's wound and doing a good professional job of bandaging it, the doctor testily agreed with Parry and Redfern that they'd had no choice but to seal the hard-bleeding cut by rough cautery. It was a godawful messy way of treating any wound, and he couldn't do much of a repair job on the seared tissue. Linc would bear a large, ugly scar to his grave. But the arm was saved, it should heal up all right, and most important, the boy would live.

Tom Redfern told Parry to stay there and look in on his family, while Redfern himself went over the ground around the Kane home. Mast and his captive had seemed to vanish into thin air, but maybe he could pick up some track. Parry nodded, dazed.

At the rear of Costiner's house was a long log building that served as a hospital when the need arose. It was staffed by Mrs. Byrne, the elderly widow of the physician who'd served the medical needs of Chinook Basin for twenty years before Costiner's arrival three years ago. Leah and Kate had been brought there at once, and after tending their injuries, Costiner had also moved Tim and Alder Kane to the hospital. Kate and Alder now occupied one of the building's four rooms, the Parry boys another, Leah a third and Nils Nansen a fourth.

"Will . . . you have to find her. You . . ."

"Sure, Lee. We'll bring her back, Tom and me. You rest now. Don't try to talk any more."

"Tom . . . ?" Leah whispered.

Glazed and dull, her eyes questioned him. Sitting at her bedside, Parry was holding her hand. He squeezed it a little tighter.

"Sure. Tom Redfern. You met him years ago, remember? He said he was coming to help us. Well, now he's here and he and I are riding out together. We'll get her back."

Leah blinked and formed a painful smile. A great purple bruise covered the swollen side of her face where Mast had hit her.

"Yes. I tried, Will . . . tried to stop him."

"I know. Don't talk any more."

"Tried so hard . . ." Leah's eyes closed and her drugged voice drifted away. "Even went up those stairs . . . two steps at a time . . . dreadfully indecorous of me. You know what Mother would say . . . ?"

Leah's head tipped sideways. She was asleep, her lips a little parted, sighing deeply. For a while at least, she would be out of it. Thank God.

Mother would have said a well-bred lady doesn't go up a stairway two steps at a time.

Parry's eyes stung as he silently finished the thought for her. Gently he detached his hand from hers and folded her arm across the blanket that covered her. From the doorway at his back, Dr. Costiner quietly cleared his throat. Parry stood up and sidled out of the room, closing the door behind him.

"Nils is awake," murmured Costiner. "No concussion, I reckon. But pretty close to it. That was a damn mean wallop he got fetched."

Parry nodded, scraping his palm over his unshaven jaw. He felt numb through and through, like a man hit over and over with hammerblows that kept driving him back and down, into an abyss of despair.

"He wants to talk to you," Costiner said.

"All right."

Parry entered the room where Nils Nansen lay on a narrow cot. His attractive wife, Ilse, sat beside him. His sixteen-year-old son, Ivar, stood by the foot of the cot.

Ilse and Ivar said formally, at the same time, "*Hur mar du*, Herr Parry?"

Parry politely inclined his head to each of them, then looked at Nils. The big blacksmith's face was pale, blanched of its usual hearty ruddiness, and he raised a hand and smiled weakly.

"Dr. Costiner has told me how it has gone with you, old hoss," he whispered. "At least you are walking about yet, eh?"

"Nils, I'm sorry about this. Damn it, I—"

"Huh!" Nils grunted, wincing as he stirred his head from side to side on the pillow. "Let's have no more talk about that, Will. Poor Wilsie . . . he is dead. If a man deals into a friend's troubles, he must take what comes. Nobody made him do it, eh?"

"No," Parry said wearily. "I guess not."

"You damn bet not." Frowning, Nils moved his gaze to

the hook on Parry's arm stump. "Ain't been using my contraption, have you?"

Parry smiled wryly. "It's been a little too much for me right now, Nils. Pretty complicated. Too many other things on my mind. Later on, all right?"

"No," Nils said. "As to most of it, maybe that's so. But Costiner says you and this friend of yours, what is his name . . ."

"Redfern. Tom Redfern."

"*Ja*, you two are going to go after Josey Mast by yourselves. Maybe that is how to do it. All right. But damn it, Will, there is all the difference in the world between the range of a pistol and a rifle. Using a rifle, a man has got every advantage. You can have it with my contraption. Where is it?"

Parry said it was in his saddlebag and Nils told him to bring it here now, right away, and bring a rifle, too, and he would explain all over how a one-handed man should use it to shoot a rifle, and dammit, Will should listen to him close this time. . . .

Redfern soon returned to tell Parry that he'd picked up a little sign left by Mast, enough to fix the direction of his flight. They ought to ready their outfits and get on the trail while it was still fresh.

Parry agreed. He took an awkward farewell of his two sons, and of Alder Kane.

Against Costiner's angry objection, Kane had insisted on getting back on his feet, as weak and shaky as he was. He knew that his remaining time was being whittled slowly away by the two serious heart attacks and a series of small strokes. He'd suffered another of the latter because of what had happened to Kate.

But, Alder Kane said, he was damned if he was going to exit this life while just sitting on his ass doing nothing.

When his time came to go, he wanted to be in harness . . . doing as much as he could still manage to do.

That might still be a good damned bit, Kane insisted in a voice that was slurred but firm. He would be on hand when the possemen came to rendezvous this morning at his place. No way of telling for sure whether Mast might not circle back here and strike again.

"I'll post men all around the hospital," Kane told Parry and Redfern. "I'll set up a cordon that even a grayback louse couldn't break through. And this time, by God, I'll oversee the whole thing myself. Meantime, you boys had best lose no time getting on the track."

Parry didn't try to argue with him. He had the glum knowledge, as they shook hands and said their good-byes and wished each other luck, that it might be the last time he and this old man he deeply admired would ever speak together.

Another thought came to him, too, and he didn't voice this one aloud either. Considering what he and Redfern were going up against, it might be Alder Kane and not Will Parry who would outlive their parting by a long while. . . .

CHAPTER SIXTEEN

Parry and Redfern rode toward the high country
that formed the eastward side of Chinook Basin where it
was rimmed by the tall peaks of the Neversummer Range.

The land climbed steadily as they went on. Redfern had
no trouble picking out the track left by Mast's horse. Or
rather, by Linc's mount on which he had made his escape
yesterday. The animal was now carrying the double burden
of Mast and Ariel. But that wouldn't matter to Mast,
Redfern observed. Plainly he was in no hurry. As always,
he was contemptuously unconcerned about anyone being
able to overtake him. Unless he chose to let them.

"He's leavin' sign as plain as day for us to follow,"
added Redfern. "If he wanted to, he could fox us off the
track with all kinds of tricks."

Parry said dully, "Not hard to figure why, is it?"

Redfern shook his head ruefully. "He knows it'll narrow
down to just us, you and me, comin' after him now. All
them posse boys of yours, they might take up the chase
again or they might not. He don't know and he don't care."

"No. He can dodge around them any way he wants."

"Sure. He's figured on what you and me will do and
we're doing it. Goin' after him by ourselves. No other
way . . . even if we know he'll lead us into a trap of some
kind. He'll sure as hell try, anyway. We got to watch out
sharp, Will."

Parry rubbed his left hand absently over the awkward cylinder of Nils Nansen's contraption, which he'd attached to his arm stump. Nils had been at pains to show him just how it should be used to help steady and fire a rifle. *It could save your life, Will,* Nils had argued. *Because this Mast guy won't expect nothing like it.* Gud *damn, it could just save your life!*

That was more than possible, Parry had conceded. Nils's vehemence alone would have half-persuaded him, even if the few practice efforts he'd made with the contraption—mock-firing a rifle under Nils's grim supervision—hadn't been reasonably convincing. Though it wasn't the same as actually using the device to aim and fire a weapon under God-knew-what conditions he'd have to face.

Still, Parry knew, the simple but versatile hook he usually wore would be of no help against an armed enemy . . . except at close quarters. Mast might not be inclined to give him any chance of that sort. So Parry had strapped on Nils's contraption once more.

Overhead, the sun had been fading out of the early morning sky. By now it had a stark, gray-steel look. Redfern tipped up his head and sniffed the air.

"Cap'n . . . Will, I think she might be building up to a hellsmear of a storm before the day is out. This time of year, that could mean rain or snow or sleet. You know the country better'n I do. What's your feeling?"

Parry sighed and shook his head. "Likely Bill Soholt could tell you, Tom. Or Linc could. Afraid I never had a sound feel for weather signs. Maybe we'll be lucky."

"Yeah," muttered Redfern. "Or we might get us a good storm that'll wipe out the track. We better hope she just holds off."

They rode on. The country became more rugged as it gained height. At first Redfern had held to the trail without leaving his horse, just leaning deeply out of his saddle once in a while, enough to pick up sign. Now the tracking was more difficult. Often Tom had to call a halt so that he could dismount and study the ground.

They made no stop at noon. At this slow pace, neither the men nor their horses needed rest. Along with blankets and slickers and some trifles of camp gear, they had packed along a supply of thick beef sandwiches, hastily put up for them by Mrs. Byrne. They munched on a few of these without leaving their saddles, washing down mouthfuls of food with swallows of water from their canteens.

Mostly they exchanged little talk as they rode. Redfern concentrated on the trail. Parry was occupied with a worry that he kept fighting back, while he pummeled his mind for anything he knew that might help them anticipate what lay ahead. Ultimately all his thinking came against a blank wall. Mast was simply too unpredictable in his actions.

They made one brief halt to get off their horses, hunker down and talk things over.

Parry said he was reasonably sure that Mast had a kind of central retreat, a well-hidden place where he could lie up when he chose, and where he could cache the food and other items he'd scavenged from ranches and stores. Granted, he might have several such caches in scattered places. Whichever, the posses had been unable to locate any cache in all their searchings.

"Well," Redfern said, "he's got a place he's heading for, all right. We can say that for sure. He's been rangin' off a straight line some, maybe to keep you and me guessin'. More'n likely, though, I'd reckon he just wants to keep us on soft ground where we can track him easy. Whatever the case, he is tending in a general direction."

"You think so?"

"Yeah." Along the way Redfern had been constantly taking out his pocket compass to check their bearings. Now he did so again, then looked at Parry and nodded. "He is holding generally east by northeast. And always toward higher land. What's up ahead of us, Will? Living hereabouts all this time, you ought to have a pretty good idea of *that* by now."

The hint of reproof in his tone made Parry smile faintly, wryly.

"I guess I know Chinook Basin well enough, Tom. The way we're headed will take us maybe three miles or so north of my own range. Mostly, around here, we don't pay too much attention to boundary lines. But if we keep going this way, we're sure to hit the Buckhorn River. It runs along my east boundary. North of my outfit, where the Buckhorn comes out of the mountains, it cuts through the roughest country anywhere about. All of it crags and canyons and hanging cliffs."

"Kind of country a lone man could lose himself in real easy, huh?"

Parry nodded. "I had our men comb it over as well as they could. But it's about like trying to hunt a human needle in a rock haystack."

"M'm. Well, it seems that's where he is taking us, for certain." Redfern snapped down the lid of his compass and gave the sky, now full of dark, scudding clouds, a long study. He shook his head once, tucked the compass back in his pocket, and then rose off his haunches. "Time we got hustling along. . . ."

The country grew even rougher as they advanced. It was studded with gigantic outcrops and boulders. But always Mast's trail clung to aisles of soft soil that took his track easily. Any of a score of places along the way would have been ideal for him to lay an ambush, and they rode with a nerve-strung awareness of this, always on the watch.

Ahead of them, before long, Parry saw the beetling rim of a ridge that he knew ran north and south for miles. Just beyond, paralleling the east escarpment, was the Buckhorn

River. Along this upper stretch it came boiling out of the mountains with a choked fury at being confined between towering rock walls. But it was wide enough to cut off any further flight in this direction.

Mast would have choices. He could lose himself in a maze of heights and ravines. Or, if he got on the rimrock, working up onto it by a less precipitous route, he could settle down to wait and pick off his pursuers as they came in sight. (Not likely: that would be too easy.) Or he could strike north or south along the base of the escarpment. (Also not likely, because why would he lead them here just to make a right-angle turn either way?)

Parry said his thoughts aloud.

Redfern pulled to a halt, rubbing his jaw speculatively. "Well, that's so. If he knows this chunk of range real good, and it's a fair bet he does, he didn't bring us here just to cut away from it. Or to get himself boxed up against the river. Whatever's in his mind, we got to figure he's bound to lay for us right soon. Any ideas?"

"None that are worth a damn, Tom. I've never explored those heights. All I know is they're a crumbling, broken-up mass of rock. Also there's a big wide-open stretch ahead of 'em. We'll have to cross it. You can't see it from here. But it's a perfect place to deadfall us if he takes a mind."

"M'm . . ." Redfern looked at the storm-brewing sky. Its overlay of clouds had turned to black-gray billows, roiling and wind-driven now. Cold gusts of wind peeled off the heights. "Now that sure looks and feels like rain to me. One helldimmer of a blow, too, or I miss my guess. Any way we can work around that open stretch?"

"None I know of." Parry swung his arm. "Those flats run way north and south along the base of the ridge, maybe a mile or so either way, from where we are now. We'd have to cut off from the track we're on."

"Unh. And no sure way of picking it up again."

"No. Even then, no matter how we tried to work up onto the ridge, we'd still be in the open a lot of the time. If he was laid up in the right place, he could take us at a walk."

Parry didn't have to add what they both knew. That Mast had appropriated both Nils's and Wilsie's rifles when he had overcome them.

Redfern sighed, reaching back to his cantle to unfasten the slicker that was lashed there. "And the storm will break way before we could manage it. That 'ud take care of any track. And we'd lose a lot of time. So instead we keep straight on his trail and take our chances."

Tom didn't add the obvious, either. That on the open place they'd be sitting ducks and it was insane to take such a chance. Except for one thing: Mast had Ariel. And he wasn't likely to take time out to do her any harm as long as a couple of pursuers were pressing him close and his first passion was to keep playing his miserable damned game with them. So they couldn't afford the least delay.

Redfern shrugged into his slicker. "Let's hustle."

Parry was already removing his own slicker from his cantle and now he pulled it on awkwardly. As an afterthought, before he buttoned it up, he dug his hook attachment out of a saddlebag and fastened it to his belt. Maybe it wouldn't be a damned bit of use, but some hunch or instinct told him to keep it on his person. . . .

In another hundred yards or so, the jumble of outcrops and boulders gave way to the stretch of flats. It was broad and regular, covered with a flinty strewing of rock chips. Looking to either side, you couldn't make out how far it extended. Up ahead, though, it was roughly three hundred yards across, and the dark wall of cliffs rose abruptly just beyond, seamed and broken, jagged along their summits.

Redfern, in the lead, looked over his shoulder at Parry. Cold flicks of wind snapped the brim of his low-pulled hat up and down. Beneath it his pale eyes held a wry simmer of excitement.

"Well, the track ends right here. He went either way or he went straight ahead. We gamble he went straight on, hunh?"

Parry only nodded. He'd forgotten how flint-strewn these flats were. He hadn't given a thought to the near-certainty that nothing could be tracked across them. But Mast would have had that thought very much in mind.

Now he moved his gaze across the jagged clifftops. Mast might be somewhere up there now, watching their approach. Nothing to be seen along the rimrock . . . no hint of movement. Why should there be? *He'll show himself when he's ready.*

Redfern nodded too, slowly. "He'll figure on all our thinkin'. If he's going to spring a trap, I reckon it'll be right here. But we might fetch him a little surprise."

"What's that?"

Still looking back at Parry, making no movement with either hand, Redfern tipped his head gently to the right, then to the left. "Along the bottom of the wall there's plenty of tumbledown rock. We'll head right for there. Give us cover of a sort if we can make it. And, Will . . . we'll ride like the devil's on our heels."

"Devil's up ahead, not at our backs," Parry murmured.

"That's right." The frosty smile of a professional manhunter, a cold pleasure that he might not even be aware of himself, touched Redfern's lips. "So let's see if we can fetch him a turn."

Parry stared at the tumble of loose rock along the distant cliff base. A cover of sorts . . . *and how much chance do we have of making it?*

"Listen," Redfern said. "Back before you lost your wing, you do any huntin'?"

"That was a long time ago."

"Sure. There's somethin' you might have forgot. Shootin' a rifle on a level is one thing. Shootin' downhill or uphill is something else. Tricky business. Hard to get a range on your target, right?"

Parry nodded.

"Right. And with a fast-movin' target, it's next to impossible. You might need two-three shots to get your range and then it might be too late, 'cause you've spooked your game and it's on the run."

"All right, Tom. I see it. We don't give him any easy-moving target to throw down on."

"That's it. Fetch him quite a start if he's looking for us to come on cautious and slow. And once we're in them rocks, we're on even terms with him. *If* he's up there, he had to leave his horse some'eres and work up *on foot*. We can do that, too."

Being above them, Mast would still have a profound advantage. But Redfern was right. If they were to force a swift confrontation, there was no other way. Despite the chill wind, Parry felt the ooze of sweat under his clothes.

"We can do that," he agreed. "Sure."

Redfern's eyelids crinkled at the corners; his smile held a brief warmth now. "You're a damn good man, Will. Case I don't get another chance to say it. You ready?"

"Ready."

Redfern yelled, *"Let's go!"* He drummed his heels against his horse's flanks, launching the animal into a run.

Parry raced after him, both men flattened to their horses' necks. The rattle of slippery flints clanging away under shod hooves made Parry suddenly aware of how perilous an all-out run was on this littered ground.

Maybe that hadn't entered even into Redfern's calculations. Or had it? He was too seasoned not to size up all odds . . . but it would also be second nature for one in his profession to run a reckless risk if the stakes warranted it.

Redfern didn't hesitate in his straining dash toward the fallaway rubble. Parry was close on his heels.

They covered a hundred yards . . . two hundred. They were less than a third of the distance from the rocks when a rifle spoke.

The bullet kicked up a fan of flinty soil just feet ahead of Redfern's racing mount. But that wasn't what drew a savage curse from him.

Both men saw the source of the shot at once. A smudge of powdersmoke was tattering off on the wind . . . but it didn't come from above. It bloomed from a nest of the tumbled rocks along the foot of the cliff and close ahead of them.

They were running into the teeth of gunfire on an open level. . . .

Redfern veered hard to the right without slackening his pace, and Parry did the same. Now they were not only close to Mast, they were broadside to him, a pair of clean targets in easy range.

And then, at the sharpest arc of its turn, Redfern's horse lost footing on the slick flints. Its hooves skidded wildly, forelegs buckling. With a terrified whicker the animal crashed sidelong on its right shoulder.

Redfern had kicked free of his stirrups at the last moment, flinging himself away from his falling mount. He landed heavily on his side, rolled over twice, and lay face-down, gasping and stunned. Parry had to wrench hard on his reins to veer wide of the fallen man, and then he pulled his horse up short.

Redfern floundered dazedly to his hands and knees, shaking his head. Mast sent off three more shots, rapid fire, gouging up geysers of sharp pebbles to either side of Redfern. His booming laugh drifted from the clump of rocks.

Clear in the open, exposed to Mast's fire, Parry froze in a

brief and brittle rush of panic. Another cluster of heavy rock lay a few yards to his right. He could reach its safety in moments. The notion gave only a fleeting tug at his mind. Then he was piling awkwardly off his horse, starting toward Redfern.

But Redfern was already stumbling to his feet. Fiercely he waved Parry back, then lunged toward his own horse. The terrified animal was getting its forehooves under it, scrambling upright. Momentarily, its shuddering effort brought the horse between them and Mast's gun.

Redfern yanked his rifle from the saddle scabbard and whirled, yelling at Parry, "Never mind the horses. Get to them rocks!"

CHAPTER SEVENTEEN

They didn't at once realize that Mast had herded them into a cul-de-sac. Nor, even after they knew it for sure, could they be certain that he'd planned it that way.

All Parry and Redfern had in mind at the moment was scrambling for the nearest rocks, escaping from the hail of lead that Mast was pumping off as fast as he could lever his rifle. Even if they had a kind of paralyzed awareness that he was shooting to scare them, not score a hit, the spatter of rock chips against their legs and a deafening clatter of echoes that showered off the cliffs was enough to keep them running fast, bent to a half crouch, till they could dive behind cover.

After that the shooting slacked off abruptly. The two men huddled among the rocks, peering out just enough to let their eyes range along the cliff base, searching out the place where Mast had lain in wait for them.

Redfern was swearing in a steady, monotonous way. Mostly he cursed himself for not having anticipated that Mast might have hidden in the fallaway rocks, not up above.

Now, he could easily fade back out of sight and go at them another way. But how to tell what the crazy bastard had in mind next?

Around this bunch of rocks every side lay open to the

flats. Except at their backs, where a narrow cleft yawned in the cliff, as if a giant wedge had split it from top to bottom.

"There's our way out o' this," Redfern said. "*If* it's a way out. Got to get higher up, Will. If we got any chance at all, it's to get up above him. He'll figure the same. Let's move."

It was a hell of a chore working their way through the gap, for it tapered down to a V-shaped apex at the bottom. Luckily the V was choked yard-deep with chunky rubble over which they slowly and laboriously clambered, Redfern in the lead.

Tom had his rifle. Parry could only wish bitterly that he'd had the presence of mind to seize his own from the saddle boot—actually Linc's rifle, borrowed for this outing in the hope he might use it to advantage with Nils's contraption. Now the hollow iron cylinder was useless except for bracing himself against the rock wall, setting up small clanking echoes as he inched along.

Ahead of them grew a faint roar of rushing water. Between the jagged walls they could see a split of open sky above another rim of cliffs that, Parry knew, marked the far bank of the Buckhorn River. It seemed an inordinately long time before they emerged from the gap onto a cliffside ledge.

Fifty feet below, the brown torrent of the Buckhorn plunged and creamed between its tall, cramping walls.

Redfern turned his head one way, then the other. He said inaudibly, "Jesus," his lips shaping the word.

To the right of them was nothing but a straight drop to the water. On their left, the shelving ledge ran along the cliff, following its uneven contour till the ledge was lost to sight around the corner of a massive bulge.

No way of telling from here whether the shelf would bend downward or upward, or whether it might offer a way for them to ascend to the rim. But it seemed to form a trail of sorts.

Redfern shouted, "Come on!" above the roar of water.

They picked their way gingerly along the ledge trail to their left. The shelf was wide enough, but the rotted granite grated crumblingly, treacherously, under their boots, making them wonder if it might give way at the next step. Cautiously they slipped around the bulge of rock that had blocked their view. What they saw ahead made their hearts sink.

The ledge trail gradually pinched off to a narrow strip and then ribboned away to nothing. Above them and below them, the walls were almost a perpendicular drop.

This was the cul-de-sac.

Redfern put his mouth close to Parry's ear and raised his voice. "We got to go back! No choice!"

"Back to what?" Parry yelled.

"Who the Christ knows what! Maybe the bastard jiggered us into this on purpose! Maybe"—Redfern nodded upward—"so he could get us from up there! Dump some rock down on us! By God, that 'ud suit him fine!"

Parry craned his neck, tipping his head back. He felt a cold jog in his belly. They were standing below a smooth line of barely sloping wall that reached to the rimrock about a hundred feet above.

God, yes. That was exactly the kind of ploy that would appeal to Josey's stunted mentality. Just about any schoolboy's favorite stunt was rolling rocks off a steep drop, for the sheer pleasure of watching them bounce and crash their way to the bottom, doing some harmless damage along the way. Did boys or men ever outgrow the mildly destructive fun of that pastime? Often enough, out with his sons, Parry had joined them in piling off their horses and bouncing boulders down steep declivities for the gleeful hell of it.

With Josey Mast—the act would take on a sadistic

dimension that froze an ordinary man to the marrow just thinking on it.

A cord of lightning writhed across the sky. A crash of thunder came racketing on its heels, the sound caroming between the cliffs. Parry could swear he felt the ancient granite quake under his feet.

"Storm's about to break!" shouted Redfern. "Let's get back . . . hurry it up!"

The two men hugged the wall as they edged back along the ledge, skirting carefully the bulge of cornering rock. Swinging around it, they came to a stop.

Josey Mast was crouched on the shelf some yards in front of the V-cleft that gave out onto it. Now he sprang to his feet, flipping away the lighted match he held. In the same movement, almost faster than the eye could follow, he was yanking a revolver from his belt, bringing it up to bear on them.

It took both Parry and Redfern a few stunned moments to realize what Mast had done.

The rough cliffside was pitted by lateral crevices. Into one such natural socket at the level of the trail, Mast had thrust a cartridge of dynamite. Its protruding end was capped and fused. Now the fuse was lighted, throwing off a sizzle of sparks.

Mast held the revolver on them, eyes lined along the sights.

"Hey there, men!" he roared. "Not 'zactly what you was looking for, unh?"

Not exactly! Mast had stolen dynamite, but who could figure what crazy twist a brain like his might take? God . . . had he had something like this in mind all along? Or was he improvising on an immediate situation? Either way—a charge of dynamite would wipe out the ledge . . . and probably bring a large section of the cliff crashing down.

Parry's mind digested the fact in a second flat. Both he and Redfern stood frozen to the spot.

"Now you shuck them guns!" Mast bellowed. "Tom, drop your rifle! *Now!*"

Redfern's jaw clenched tight. His Winchester was pointed offside, held in one hand. He hadn't had enough time to make the least move with it before Mast had them covered.

"Do it, Tom!" Mast's grin was a white smear in the black tangle of his beard.

Redfern opened his hand. The rifle clattered to the ledge.

"Now your sidearms! Throw 'em away from you! Into the river! Tom, use your left hand!"

Redfern pulled his revolver from its holster left-handed and pitched it away. Parry mechanically did the same.

Mast lowered the gun and let it off-cock, holding it at his side. He let out a wild cackle.

"Man, that's pluperfect! That's fine! Now you buckoes start backin' up! Get yourselves back around that turn o' rock! Or stand where you be and get yourselves blown from here to kingdom come!"

It was clear they had no choice. The dynamite cartridge had what Parry judged was a two-minute fuse dangling from its capped end—and it was burning down fast.

When the cartridge went off, the explosion would wipe them clean off the ledge if it didn't kill them outright. Men had been known to survive detonations in an immediate blast area. But the concussion alone would send them plunging to just as sure a death.

"Go on!" Mast roared happily. "Go on standin' right there!"

Roused into motion now, Parry and Redfern began to back up along the ledge. They cleared the swell of corner rock and pulled back around it. Then they shrank tight against the wall, waiting for the blast.

Suddenly Redfern swore. "*No*, goddammit!"

He lunged forward and Parry grabbed his arm. *"Tom! What—?"*

"Will, if he blows out the trail, we'll be stranded here! That's what he wants! Let go!"

Redfern gave a savage jerk of his arm, pulling free of Parry's grip. He swung around the rock bulge and Parry, taking a few steps after him, saw him vault along the ledge to reach the sputtering charge of dynamite.

Josey Mast wasn't in sight. He'd already retreated back into the sheltering V-cleft. Redfern tripped in his run and fell to his hands and knees. At once he scrambled back to his feet. In a half-dozen more floundering strides, he almost reached the sizzling fuse. He made a dive for it.

Too late.

Parry shrank back instinctively, hugging the granite bulge as the dynamite went off. He had only a fleeting glimpse of the scene as everything dissolved in a thunderous fury.

The whole massive formation trembled as if pulverized to the core. Parry was deafened by the rumble of falling rock as it scaled away from the cliff face and cascaded into the water below.

None of it came down where he was standing. After a few seconds (though it seemed an agonizingly longer time), the reverberations ceased. Parry felt a sick thud of blood pounding around his heart as he edged back to the bulging corner of rock.

An immense layer of the cliffside had been ripped away. With it had gone a large section of the ledge trail. A vast slide of rubble choked the narrow channel of the river below. Already the pent-up water was boiling up behind it, backing up till it could pour past the obstruction.

The avalanche had taken Redfern with it, burying him under a splintered mass of debris.

A haze of powdery dust was still settling over the scene.

Parry moved mechanically forward along the ledge, coughing. As the dust thinned away, he saw Mast emerge from the cleft and come toward him, grinning.

"Hey, Cap'n!" Mast shouted. "That plumb tears the rag offen the bush for sure! Didn't mean to fetch ol' Tom jus' that way . . . but I reckon it's about as sure as any!"

Parry stared at his enemy across the wide gap between them, where maybe fifteen feet of the ledge trail had been blown away.

Mast's face was a shocking sight. It had a raw and broiled look and his mashed nose was a crusted scab. Forming a grin was causing him considerable pain, pulling his bearded lower face out of skew into a puckered and hideous leer.

The man's primal malignancy reached across to Parry like an evil vapor. It tore loose a last restraint in him. All the boiling hatred and tension of these last long days erupted from him in a raging yell.

"Mast, you bastard! What did you do with my girl!"

Mast let out a booming whinny of a laugh. He stood with his legs apart, his tattered clothes streaming out on the cold wind.

"Not a goddam thing, Cap'n! Yet! I got 'er tucked away back in a place yonder. . . ." Mast waved a hand toward the north. "But I sure gonna do plenty now! Then I'm gonna tell you 'bout what I done, unh? When I do"—he pointed at the rimrock above Parry's head—"I'll be bouncing down a few rocks at you. I'll tell you all 'bout your girlie and me whilst you're dodging rocks! How's 'at set in your craw!"

Parry felt as if his legs had turned to water, his knees threatening to fold under him. He steeled his will, holding himself straight up, as he stared back at Mast. One slim hope brushed his mind now. But for the moment—unarmed, helpless, the enemy he couldn't touch just a few yards away—he just looked back at Mast with a pure and iron-faced hatred.

Mast stood as he was, grinning. Maybe he hoped for another display of raw feeling.

When it didn't come, he raised one hand in idle salute and then, still grinning, turned on his heel and sauntered back toward the V-passage.

With Mast's back to him, Parry seized on the one remaining chance he had.

The river's roar covered the sounds he made running forward along the ledge to grab up Redfern's rifle. He braced it to his right shoulder with his one hand, nestled the stock to his jaw and took aim between Mast's shoulders.

Big Nils had shown him just how the "contraption" could be used, and Parry had tested it with Linc's rifle. Clumsy as it was, it would do the job on a not-too-distant target . . . maybe. An attachment on the cylinder that capped his right arm enabled Parry to grasp the Winchester's stock and pull the hammer back to cock, the two actions being simultaneous. On the cylinder's end a tiny metal hook would enable him, with the slightest shift of his grip, to pull the trigger.

But it was damned awkward. And Mast was almost at the mouth of the passage. . . .

There was no time to squeeze off his shot carefully. Parry jerked the trigger. And knew even as he fired that the gun barrel was skewing sideways, his aim spoiled.

Mast grunted and heaved forward on his toes, half turning under the bullet's force. He staggered forward a few steps, then swung fully around, his right hand gripping his left arm. His red scalded face was snarling. Blood soaked his ragged sleeve.

Hastily, even as Mast turned, Parry levered and cocked the Winchester. He jerked off another shot. It went totally wide of the mark, the slug screaming off a rock abutment.

"Hey . . . that's really somethin' now!" Mast's voice grated like a rusty saw. "But not damn good enough!"

He drew his revolver in a blurred motion, cocked and raised it. From where he stood, maybe thirty feet away, he could take his time fixing an easy, almost point-blank bead on his adversary. Parry's whole body braced for the slug's impact. But Mast didn't fire. With a noiseless laugh he dropped the gun back in its holster.

"You wait right where you be, Cap'n! This skeeter bite you fetched me ain't gonna slow me by one little lizard turd! Soon's I've tended to your girlie, I'll be back to see to you!"

As he spoke, Mast took a long sideways step into the cliff passage. It swallowed him from sight.

The rifle slipped out of Parry's hands. He sank down on his haunches, sick and shaking. He was marooned on this ledge. Stuck fast on the cliffside as helpless as a cripple-winged bird. *Ariel! Oh Christ!*

Lightning ripped across the sky. The first fat drops of rain began to pelt down, striking with an oddly warm sensation on his icy face and hands.

CHAPTER EIGHTEEN

Ariel RETURNED TO HER SENSES BY DEGREES, SLOWLY AND painfully.

At first only a sludge of impressions stirred in her mind, shapeless blurs of brown and gray. As they rolled away and she came fully awake, a soft cry of pain gurgled in her throat.

The cry was muffled by the heap of smelly blankets on which she was sprawled, facedown. Then she realized that her hands were tied behind her and her feet were lashed together. She could barely move a muscle; when she tried, the attempt sent waves of agony through her head and body.

In the first panicked thrust of waking up, Ariel's mind clutched wildly at tag ends of memory.

The last thing she could recall clearly was Josey Mast's big fist coming at her face. A crush of pain and sudden darkness. That was right after she'd seen the same fist smash her mother into unconsciousness.

The next thing she'd known was a drifting awareness of jogging along belly-down across a horse's forequarters, a saddle horn digging cruelly into her middle. A man was in the saddle and she was slung across it in front of him. All she could make out was his ragged trouser leg and a moccasined foot in stirrup and the dark ground moving below her. She'd let out a feeble croak and then retched, vomiting over Mast's foot. He had sworn once and then slugged her in the head, probably with his fist again.

Afterward Ariel had roused a little from time to time, to vague patches of consciousness, fleeting and uncertain.

She knew only that she was carried a long, long way in the same brutally punishing position . . . that the sky was lightening to an overcast dawn . . . finally that Mast was bearing her across his shoulder as he toiled up a long, rocky escarpment. Then all motion ceased. Mercifully, she was no longer being jolted about like a sack of meal. She had sunk into an oblivion of sleep.

Now, moaning sickly against the battering ache of her head, the soreness of her bruised body—really painful where the saddle horn had gouged her belly—Ariel managed to turn her head sideways, getting her face out of the stinking blankets.

Was she in a cave of some sort?

No. It seemed to be just a shallow nook in a hillside or something. Roughly twelve feet square, it was less than six feet high from sandy floor to rock ceiling. An overhang slab shelved downward above its narrow mouth, affording some shelter from weather . . . and maybe from searching men who had failed to look closely enough. It faced out on a darkish vista of broken rock under a sky of tumbling gray clouds.

Biting deeply into her underlip, steeling herself for the effort, Ariel rolled onto her back.

Lordy God, she hurt all over. She was clad only in her torn and crumpled nightgown. The air around her throbbed warmly and not unpleasantly through the cotton fabric clinging to her damp flesh. Yet now she felt chill gusts of wind starting to flick in and out of the nook. It felt like a storm was coming up. . . .

She shivered with more than cold as she peered dazedly around her. Light reached dimly into the nook, but she could make things out clearly enough. Yes. This was Josey Mast's hidden camp.

A heap of dead ashes lay close to the opening. Ariel had a sluggish memory of her father and Alder Kane speculating that wherever Mast was laid up, he wouldn't chance a cookfire out in the open that might be spotted after dark. And he wouldn't make giveaway smoke by day.

A raw smoke smell clung to the whole interior of the nook, particularly to the blankets that must have soaked it up like water. It mingled with other evil stenches that were less definable but just as stifling. And sickening. *Lordy God . . . what a bear's den!*

A lot of miscellaneous gear was stacked along the walls, enough to stock the crude and temporary quarters of a fugitive who reckoned to be stuck here for quite a spell. Such things as an ax, a bridle, a pile of rawhide cords, a roll of wire, some tarp-wrapped bundles that might contain stores of food. An odd assortment of weapons—a couple of rifles and some revolvers along with several knives—was laid in a neat row on a spread-out rubber slicker to shield it from damp ground.

There was a wooden box from which, it looked like, the top had been ripped away hastily. The splintered top leaned against the crate and she saw that it bore black-stenciled lettering:

> DANGER
> HIGH EXPLOSIVES
> THIS SIDE UP
> NO. 1 DYNAMITE $1\frac{1}{2} \times 8$ IN.

Mast had dumped her here, left her tied up, then had gone away. How long ago? She didn't know. It might have been minutes . . . or hours. Where had he gone? She had no idea. Why had he gone? Likely to watch against a pursuit. The posses would be out . . . on his trail. If he had left any kind of a trail. Thus far, she knew, they hadn't picked up any.

Terrified as she was, hurting all over, Ariel forced her mind to work coolly now. A pure instinct to survive held back most of her panic.

Getting her hands free. That must come first.

She fixed her attention on the two hunting knives and the one ordinary kitchen butcher knife that gleamed among the layout of Mast's guns. If she could get one of those in her hands, maybe she could accomplish it. *Before he comes back!*

Gritting her teeth, Ariel heaved up into a sitting position. She hitched herself gradually around on the sand floor and, digging in her bare heels, edged over to the spread of weapons on the slicker. Fumbling backward, she closed her fist over the handle of the butcher knife. Thin and finely honed, it would be best for the purpose. Her fingers were so numbed by the bite of the thongs around her wrists that she could barely manage to grasp it.

Suddenly a volley of shots reached her ears. Ariel tensed, listening. But the shooting tapered off quickly. *What did it mean?*

Slowly and awkwardly, fear boiling in her belly, she propped the knife between her hands so that the blade angled upward. Then she began to saw slowly and clumsily at the rawhide cords. If only they were green thongs! But they were hard and flinty, toughly seasoned against her necessarily feeble efforts. Straining her head around, she could see that the blade was denting the thongs with an agonizing slowness.

Oh God help me . . . please!

Thunder boomed, suddenly and powerfully. From her narrow vantage, Ariel could see no flash of lightning. But the storm was coming on fast.

Twice as she cut, Ariel felt the blade slip from the cords

and slice into her flesh. She felt a warm slickness of blood on her hands. She tasted a salty warmth of blood on her underlip where her teeth bit into it.

Once she paused as a deep roar came from some distance away, reverberating through the earth. It wasn't like a thunderboom . . . and she stared at the open case of explosives. She knew the sound of a dynamite blast. But where—*or at what*—would Mast be blasting?

Careful . . . slow . . . just keep trying. Oh God help me!

Her neck ached from craning her head to watch the knife's progress. Suddenly the blade was cutting deeper, the strands beginning to part.

She saw a tongue of lightning lick down with a clear blinding flash. The roll of thunder that followed was like a burst of cannon fire. Blobs of rain began to fall. They made dark splatters along the outside ledge of rock that protruded a few feet from below the steep overhang.

Once they started to go, the cords were quickly severed by a few furious strokes. She was almost amazed to find her hands jerking apart, bloody but alive with feeling now. A couple of quick slashes of the butcher knife freed her ankles.

Ariel pushed up off her haunches. For a moment she stood swaying on her feet, her arms and legs tingling with a rush of blood from restored circulation. A near hysterical laugh bubbled from her lips.

Her first instinct was to get out of this stinking trap of a den, to get out and away from it before *he* came back. She started toward the low opening under the overhang slab, crouching so she could duck out under it.

Another jagged ribbon of lightning flared, its white blaze lighting the whole broken-up landscape. Along with the earsplitting crack of thunder, it made her cower back, clapping both hands over her ears.

Oddly, it also helped to clear and cool her thoughts.

She was barefoot, had on nothing but a thin soiled nightdress, had no idea whatsoever just where she was. She needed some kind of footgear. And something to cover herself. *And a gun?*

Ariel dropped on her knees among the scatter of Mast's plunder and pawed through it. She found nothing to put on her feet . . . nothing to wrap around her but a blanket. Goaded by a panicked urgency now, she quickly chose one of the revolvers—a Colt double-action .45. Some time back her brother Linc had showed her how to use one, just for shooting at targets. She'd never even held a rifle—maybe she'd been affected by Ma's own aversion to them.

But Linc's casual instruction with the .45 in some idle half-forgotten hour stuck in her mind. The weapon felt almost like a talisman, a little oversize and awkward, but fitting smoothly into her palm.

Ariel crawled out of the nook. With one hand she clutched a blanket around her; the other gripped the revolver. Then she scrambled to her feet.

The slight ledge on which she stood tipped off into a steep flinty slope below. Looking up at the high rimrock above, she gathered that she was halfway up a rock escarpment. By now the silvery lances of rain were rattling down fast, hissing against surfaces of rock and obscuring much of the landscape on every side. She could make out dark gray spires of broken rock and, here and there, nondescript patches of vegetation.

Ariel began to climb downward, hugging the rocks and picking out holds with her bare feet.

Like any country-raised girl, she was used to going barefoot half the year; memories of childhood callus clung to her soles. Her toes hooked easily around whatever they could grasp onto. She knew instinctively how to relax or settle her weight as she groped her way down over the stony protuberances.

Before she reached the bottom, the rain was coming down in slashing sheets that made the blanket around her shoulders a useless, soggy encumbrance. She shrugged it away. With one hand free to help her along, her descent was faster. But she kept a tight grasp on the revolver.

Finally her feet touched the stony root of the slope. Moving out and away from it, shielding her eyes with her hand so she could peer through the rain, Ariel swiftly realized—from this lower vantage—approximately where she was.

Above her loomed the crumbling granite ridge that ran for miles along the west side of the Buckhorn, its bends and breaks guiding the river's course, holding it back from the stony lowlands beyond. Often, on hot summer days, she and her brothers would sneak off this way to go swimming. Leah had always warned them against these precipitous cliffs and the brawling rush of river, deeming it an unsafe place for kids to go prowling.

But being kids, she and Linc—and more recently Tim as well—had ignored Ma's interdict and had gone exploring the area whenever they could. Sometimes, too, they would make their way through the ridge formation, with its bust-up of crevices and rock slides, to quiet backwater loops of the river. Here they could dive and swim and dare each other to venture close to dangerous stretches of turbulence.

Ma would have had conniption fits if she'd ever found out.

Anyway, Ariel could now be sure she was on the western side of the Buckhorn. From here she knew the country well enough to pick her way across the rocky higher ground to WP's grassy west range. Afterward, taking her bearings from various landmarks, she could easily find her way to the ranch headquarters.

Right here, though, she was still in plain sight from above. Quickly Ariel struck out north along the uneven base of the escarpment, wanting to reach the closest of the granite outthrusts that would cut her off from view of anyone on the ridge.

Hobbling along as fast as she could, she winced only a little at the bite of flint on her bare soles. The warm rain plastered the thin gown to her slim nubile body and once more—oddly and incongruously in this moment of being terrified half out of her wits—she had the fleeting thought that it was really kind of a pleasant sensation. . . .

Ariel reached the half-crumbled spire of rock, ducked around the concealment of its north side and dropped on her haunches. She rested that way for a moment, her head bent against the beating rain. Cautiously then, she drew herself forward and edged her face around the rocky angle. Blinking against the rain, she peered up along the dark ridgeside she had quitted.

Oh God. There he was.

A lean dark form barely seen through the slanting veils of rain. But it had to be Josey Mast. He was loping easily down from the ridgetop above, down toward the shadowy nook where he'd cached his stores . . . and had left her tied up. He reached the opening and ducked inside.

Beyond the spire where she was hidden were other isolated outcrops. Now Ariel sprang to her feet and headed for the nearest one, maybe ten yards away. Unable to run across the broken-flint ground, she felt that the few seconds it took her to cover that distance seemed more like an eternity. She sank down behind the outcrop, gasping.

Again she cautiously peered out.

Mast was coming back out on the ledge, turning his head to left and right, conning a landscape that was shrouded by a gray obscurity of rain. Then he began to clamber down the slope, lithe as a goat, a rifle swinging in one hand. When he reached the bottom, he paused and bent down and picked something up—the soaked blanket she had discarded.

He let it fall from his hand and straightened up, holding his face to the rain, looking all around him with that animal alertness of his.

There was no track he could pick up on. That was something . . . but he could be sure she hadn't gotten very far. *If only he'd strike off in a wrong direction!*

But he didn't. As if out of some primitive intuition, he began to tramp this way along the base of the ridge.

Ariel shrank back against the outcrop.

She had hoped that a worsening storm might conceal any move she made to steal away. By now the cannonades of thunder were crashing continuously, ebbing away into low rumbles and then crashing again. But those first blinding sheets of rain had already slacked off to a steady drizzle. If she tried to run, Mast would spot her at once and overtake her in a few moments. If she remained where she was, she'd be discovered for certain . . .

That left only one thing to do.

Ariel looked at the double-action revolver in her hand. Linc had told her that the ordinary Colt wasn't worth shucks beyond a few yards away. Yellowback thrillers extolling the weapon's fabulous accuracy were nothing but hogwash. A few professional sharpshooters who were willing to burn powder for many hours just practicing could gain a fair proficiency with one. Otherwise, for any distance shooting, a body might as well be armed with a peashooter.

You can use the other hand to brace your gun hand, Linc had told her. *That helps a mite. But you still got to have time to get you a good aim. You need to pull iron on somebody real quick, you can't take much time. What you do, just try to get your shot in first and make it good.*

Ariel flexed the aching muscles of her arms, fighting back a numbness of fear. Then she stood up in the warm rain.

As she'd reckoned, Mast was very close by now, not

coming straight on toward her shelter, but near enough that he'd have been sure to discover her in another minute or so.

Now, as her head and upper body cleared the outcrop, he saw her and came to a dead stop. Ariel's arms were already extended straight out before her, the Colt in one fist, the palm of her other hand cupping and bracing it.

She fired.

The bullet made a screaming ricochet off a stone abutment in back of Mast and a couple of yards away from his right side. Firmly Ariel shifted one leg to brace her feet apart and fired again. This time the slug burst a sodden crumble of rock on the slope behind him and missed him (she vaguely judged) by less than a foot.

Still it was a miss. And she had a wild, instinctive sense that she'd pulled off both shots just a shade too quickly.

Mast let out a loud growl of a laugh. His rifle was coming up and he was taking his time.

Ariel lined her sights carefully—*please dear God!*—and tried again.

The hammer fell with a futile click. Misfire? Or moisture damping the primer? Would that happen with metal-jacketed cartridges?

She jerked the trigger twice more. Nothing.

Mast lowered his rifle now. He moved forward, his moccasined feet sloshing over the wet, flinty ground. He was coming on toward her with the oddly gaunt grace of a big, rawboned wolf.

Over the hiss of falling rain, she heard him growl happily in his throat.

"You stay right there, girlie. You do look real fine, all wet like that, you know? You jus' stay like you are. . . ."

CHAPTER NINETEEN

THE CROOKED AND NARROW LEDGE ON WHICH PARRY WAS stranded pinched away to nothing at one end. At its other end was a blown-away gap that an athlete in prime condition might be able to leap across, if he had a good running start. The remnant of ledgerock that remained was too short and irregular for a man to manage even one stride of a brief, awkward run.

After Parry's first despairing realization ebbed enough for him to think again, he knew what he would have to try.

Ordinarily it was harder for a body to climb down than up a vertical surface—any kid who'd ever shinnied up a tree knew that much—but the place where Mast's charge of dynamite had wiped out the ledge trail had also brought down the vast slide of rock that had buried Tom Redfern under it. If a man could make his way to where the treacherous slant of rubble began not too far below, and get from there down to the river's edge, he could then work upstream or downstream across a shoreline of boulders and shallow water. It would be slow going, but with any luck he might come to a place where he could climb up and out of the deep riverbed cut with comparative ease.

But Parry wasn't familiar enough with the rivercourse to be sure where there was such a place, if any. Or if there was, how long he'd be in locating it, going either down- or upstream.

Time. *Christ!* There was so little time to spare. Or—more likely—no time at all. He didn't know how far away Mast was holding Ariel and no idea where, except it was in a northerly direction. How much chance did he stand of finding them in a hurry . . . or finding them at all?

In any case, getting off this shelf as quickly as he could meant he'd have to go upward. Ascend the almost straight-up cliff to its liprock.

Even a man with two good hands would have to be out of his mind to consider trying it . . . unless he was an experienced and properly equipped climber. But a one-handed man full of a half-crazed determination, driven by a frantic need for haste, might damned well do it.

Or he could die trying.

Raindrops were pattering down faster by the moment. Lightning blazed; thunder crashed.

Parry prowled swiftly along the shelf from one end to the other, sizing up the cliff wall overhead, trying to pick out the least hazardous line of ascent. At the same time he was shedding the bulky impediment of his slicker. He also discarded Nils's cylindrical apparatus and strapped the familiar hook on his arm stump.

He quickly mapped out in his mind what might be the likeliest course up the face of the cliff . . . just beyond that angling bulge where the trail began to taper away. At that point above the ledge, the wall was almost sheer and unpitted. But it grew more rugged higher up, and then it began to slant inward a little. Parry figured that if he followed it on a zigzag upward, there'd be enough tight lateral crevices and knobby projections to offer slight holds for his feet, his hand, and his hook.

Before he could think on it any further, the storm broke in all its torrential fury.

Buffeted by wind-driven masses of rain, he had all he could do to hug the wall and not be swept from his narrow perch. He hunched his shoulders and waited for what seemed endless minutes till the lashing sheets abated enough for him to see upward again.

Rain was still cascading fiercely off the rimrock, half-blinding him.

But Parry couldn't wait any longer. He tucked his chin down, reached as high as he could, clamped his hand around a protuberance of rough granite and dragged his whole weight as far upward as the bending of his arm would allow. The rain-slick rock afforded the worst kind of hold. Still he was able to reach higher with his other arm and wedge the tip of his hook into a shallow horizontal crack.

He let go his handhold to take a still higher grip.

Instantly he felt a violent wrench at his right wrist. The leather sheath of the hook was slipping as that arm took his full weight, pulling away from the knob of bone where his wrist anchored it.

In a desperate surge Parry drew up his knees, scrabbling wildly with his boots. He managed to kick the toe of his right boot into the support of a shallow crevice.

At the same time he groped wildly for a second handhold and miraculously found it. This enabled him to hoist himself still higher. Then he dared to relax the grip of his hook arm on the crack where it was fixed. He awkwardly maneuvered the tip of his left boot into the crevice next to the right one.

Now his hand and both feet were supporting him, though damned precariously. But the leather sleeve on his right wrist had slipped nearly free.

Clinging like a fly to the pitted cliff wall, Parry savagely and clumsily hammered the curving hook against it, driving the leather jacket back on his wrist till it again caught behind the wristbone.

Peering up, he tried to single out the next possible hold he might take. Once more the silvery bursts of rain off the rim nearly blinded him and he ducked his head again. *No use.* He'd have to depend wholly on his memory of the rough surveillance he'd taken from below.

He straightened his legs as much as he could, straining onto his toes, and struck upward with the hook. At once it lodged into another crevice. He gave a tentative jerk at the hold and it felt secure. His knees were touching a small abutment that he thought might support his feet . . . if he could only reach higher.

Taking a chance, he flexed his right arm and pulled upward, letting the hook take his full weight while his straight left arm grabbed up wildly for where he believed another handhold was.

As his hand closed over a rain-slick protuberance, the hook on his other arm tore suddenly free of its leather sleeve. For a moment the whole weight of his body swung violently from that single handhold, almost wrenching away his grip on it.

He heard the hook clang downward and bounce off the rock ledge. Any further noise of its falling was lost in the din of hissing rain and roaring river.

Hanging one-handed, feeling his grasp starting to slip, Parry jacked his knees up, feeling with his toes for the shallow abutment. They found it. Slowly, testing the foothold, he straightened his legs again. It relaxed some of the strain on his hand and enabled him to hike himself a couple of feet higher.

Now what?

He had barely managed to achieve the plentifully pitted inward slant of the upper cliff. Now he'd have had much easier going—except for having lost the damned hook.

Could he make it one-handed?

No room for a single misstep or a wrong hold now. If he made one, he would follow his hook to the bottom of the long drop. He had a brief cruel image of his broken and jellied carcass on the river-edging rocks below.

With a slow and infinite care, moving just inches at a time, Parry began his painstaking crawl up the last slant of rock below the rim. Rain poured over and around him. The slow, groping holds he was able to feel out with his hand and feet were water-slick and treacherous.

Every fiber of his body ached with the effort. Pain sliced like knives into his fingers. Then he could no longer feel them. He could feel hardly anything as a dead numbness spread through his arm, his legs, his whole body.

Oh, Christ. He was going to let go for sure. When the nerve-ends were gone, the fingers would have to unbend. Then . . .

Suddenly he thought of his wife. With all her dread of guns, her hatred of violence, Leah had somehow made do to the last moment—defending her daughter like a tigress.

God *damn!*

A pure and desperate fury fed Parry's remaining strength. Once more he inched himself onward and upward.

Abruptly, mercifully, he became aware that the steep incline was sloping in toward the rimrock. He was even able to use the elbow of his handless arm to partially brace his weight and hitch himself along.

At last Parry heaved his upper body over the rounded edge of the rim. Only then did he dare to let his straining muscles go suddenly and shudderingly loose. He lay soddenly against the rimrock with his legs still dangling over the drop, resting and gasping as the rain beat steadily down on him.

Finally he pulled himself up the last few feet, got solid ground under his boots, dragged himself upright, and staggered away from the rim.

Now that he was atop the giant ridge, he felt a dull surprise at seeing how relatively regular it was along the crown. Scanning it from below, a man got the idea that its summit would be split by deep fissures, jagged with outcrops, perhaps impossible to negotiate. In fact, he saw now that although the steep-sided height was uneven and crumbling along its top, it ran fairly level along its north to south course.

Picking his way with care, he should be able to make his way along it without too much difficulty.

Mast had indicated a direction vaguely to the north. That meant he was likely holding Ariel at a place somewhere atop the ridge or along its sides. It was pitted and broken-up enough to afford plenty of hiding places that wouldn't easily be discovered except by a close observer, and such a place might also have served as Mast's provisioned center of operations. . . .

Parry allowed himself a few moments of rest, flexing his bleeding hand, feeling a slow return of strength to his numb muscles. Then he trudged northward along the ridgetop, doing his best to size up the terrain that lay ahead through the gray veil of rain.

Tongues of lightning flickered on and off, not as noisily as before. The flashes were a help in picking out his way. But a thickening despair filled him. The ridge must run from two hundred to three hundred feet wide, depending where you were located on its rambling, irregular length. On either side it might conceal hidden pockets that couldn't be spotted from above or below.

But Parry fell into luck. Maybe he'd been about due for some.

Veering in his slow progress along the western brink, he came on a deep split in the formation. Below, just inside the crevasse and somewhat sheltered from the blasts of wind and rain, he saw a hobbled horse.

Parry's heart kicked a hard beat against his ribs. Even

from this high up, he could easily identify Linc's horse on which Mast had made his escape from WP headquarters.

Then he must be close to Mast's covert. But God . . . where was it in all this maze of fissures and outcrops? Ahead or below? Maybe even somewhere along the other, river-facing side of the ridge?

He was still a man sick with apprehension, a man stumbling along a blind trail. But now he moved more warily, his senses sharpened and alert.

He heard the crash of a gunshot. Then another.

Parry scrambled over a long granite hump that lay between him and where he judged the shots had come from. Three times in his haste he fell to his hands and knees, pain shooting through his raw-scraped body, before he came in full sight of what was happening below.

Ariel was down there, standing next to a rock abutment with a revolver clasped in her extended hands. Mast was advancing on her, yelling something at her, words that Parry couldn't make out.

Momentarily she shrank backward, away from Mast, then turned and tried to run. But he was on top of her in a few seconds, grabbing her from behind, wrapping his arms around her, and bearing her to the ground.

CHAPTER TWENTY

Evidently Ariel had managed somehow to free herself, then had led Mast a chase before he'd overtaken her. Barefoot on flinty ground, she probably hadn't gotten very far. But it had bought her a little precious time. Otherwise, by now, it was almost certain Mast would have done his worst.

These thoughts passed through Parry's mind as fleeting impressions. He was already sliding over the brink of the slope, half scrambling, half falling as he plunged downward toward them at an angle. The grade wasn't very steep at this point, but the slope was littered with shards of broken granite.

Seeing Ariel struggling on the ground, Mast on top of her, Parry was heedless of any further injury to himself. He'd nearly reached the bottom when he bashed his right knee against a rock, but he was hardly aware of the pain.

He heard Ariel's faint, choked screams. The sound burned out to his nerve ends and filled his mind with one thought: *Get Mast . . . kill the bastard.*

The steady splash of rain muffled any noise of his descent. When he reached the slope's base, he was retching with the fury of his exertions. But he was still something like a hundred or more feet behind Mast and his daughter.

Parry was limping badly, almost dragging his right leg, as he hobbled doggedly toward them.

Mast's back was to him. Dimly now Parry remembered the hunting knife he kept sheathed at his left hip. The only weapon he had left.

He grasped at it twice, his mangled fingers slick with water and blood, before he could close his fingers over it and yank the knife free of its sheath.

He'd covered all but a few yards of the distance that separated him from Mast's back when some slight noise he made—or maybe pure animal intuition—caused Josey Mast to look back across his shoulder.

Mast sprang to his feet and whirled around.

Just the sight of his fierce, scalded face and the scabbed mash of his nose, all glistening wet, might have been enough to stop some men in their tracks. It only inflamed Parry. He took a last couple of hobbling steps and felt his hurt right leg cave under him as he launched himself at Mast.

Even as he made the awkward dive, Parry was falling, going down on his face within a few feet of his enemy. As he fell, he flung out his hand and took a wild and desperate slash at Mast's moccasined leg.

Mast tried to leap sideways, away from the thrust and from Ariel's prone body behind him. But not quickly enough. The knife bit into his ankle, bit deep through leather and flesh and into bone.

Mast let out a bawl of rage and pain. He stumbled and nearly fell. But managed, with his usual pantherish ferocity, to keep on his feet. His hand shot down to the belt cinched around his ragged trousers. A revolver was holstered there, also a knife protruding from its sheath.

A gray foretaste of defeat filled Parry's mouth as he floundered up on his knees and stump and hand, still awkwardly clutching his hunting knife.

Mast laughed.

He took one step and stamped savagely on Parry's hand. The fingers splayed, losing their grip on the knife's slippery handle. Then the hard upcurled toe of Mast's moccasin drove against his temple in a vicious kick.

Parry's senses pinwheeled away. He felt a raw dig of flint on his face as he sagged down. But only for an instant. Mast was grabbing a handful of his hair, yanking his head up and back.

Something snapped down over Parry's head and fastened around his neck. He felt a sear of agony in his flesh. Then something far worse: a choke of shut-off wind.

Mast was above and behind him, dragging Parry up to his knees now. His own knee was rammed into Parry's spine, arching him relentlessly backward as Mast increased the pressure.

Parry had a brief and terrifying awareness that what Mast had reached for at his belt hadn't been a gun or knife. It was the shining coil of wire that Parry had briefly glimpsed . . . maybe the same one Mast had used to snare Parry's arm in the bunkhouse, the one he had used to strangle Wilsie Manlow.

Parry gurgled in his throat as Mast yanked the wire still tighter. He did it with a deadly dexterity, chuckling crazily. "This is it, Cap'n—this here is all of it for you. . . ."

Parry clawed with his one hand at the strangling dig of wire in his throat. Futilely. Gagging against the slow crush of his windpipe, he threw his upper body from side to side. It only made the wire bite deeper. Mast's strength was enormous.

Parry's vision slipped from gray to spotty in the terrible penumbra of pain. He was starting to black away. Yet he was vaguely aware that one of Mast's hands was weakening, losing its grip. Yes, he thought dimly, why not; he had shot the son of a bitch in one arm. . . .

At the same time he had a blacking-out impression of Ariel rolling up to a crouch just ahead of him. Then she was coming up off her haunches, looking around her, reaching down, closing her hand over a fist-sized hunk of stone—

Suddenly Mast let go of the wire. Parry fell forward on his face. Instantly the wire loop that was sawing into his throat sprang free. Air gushed into his lungs; congested blood ran out of his head.

The knife he had dropped lay gleaming on the wet, dark flints just inches from his face.

Ariel let out a shriek of pain. The sound sent a fresh burst of life into Parry's numb brain, his unfeeling muscles. But he still felt like a man oddly detached from his own body as he watched his hand creep out to close over the knife hilt.

Putting out a mighty effort, he braced his fist and stump against the ground and pushed up to his knees.

Mast had seized Ariel's arm before she could brain him with the rock. Now he was twisting her arm back at a cruel angle. The rock had slipped from her fingers. Mast gave her a savage cuff, grunting with the force of it or with pure satisfaction. He swept his arm to catch her again on the backswing.

Parry was stumbling to his feet as Mast let go of the girl and let her crumple to the ground. Once more Mast's back was turned to Parry and this time he didn't wheel around fast enough.

Parry gathered the last dregs of his strength. He swung.

A glittering arc of steel caught Mast just under the armpit. The blade hammered deep and hard between his ribs. A spurt of hot blood drenched Parry's hand even as Mast gave a convulsive heave of his body that tore the knife from Parry's grasp.

Mast stumbled backward, tripped over Ariel's prone form and fell.

Parry stood as he was, swaying a little as he fought to stay upright. His brain was still dim; he had no real strength left in him.

He watched Mast roll onto his side and then, drawing on that terrible and tenacious animal vitality of his, climb back to his knees and heave back onto his feet. His long sinewy hands fumbled at the protruding knife. The heavy blade was embedded nearly to its hilt in his side.

Mast's eyes were already dulling and filming over as they lifted and fixed on Parry.

"Why," he said in a wondering and disbelieving voice, "why goddam you all t'hell, Cap'n. . . ."

He staggered a few steps backward, still clutching the knife handle. He fell to his knees, then pitched onto his face. His body was motionless in the spitting rain. . . .

Ariel sat with her back against a boulder, hugging the wet and torn nightgown to her shoulders. Her face was puffed and bruised. She was shivering a little under the slow rain. But it was dying off to a fine mizzle now.

"I'll never forget this, Daddy," she murmured. "Any of it, ever. As long as I live."

Parry was sitting on his heels a few yards from her, arms crossed on his knees, his head bowed with exhaustion. Slowly he looked up.

"None of us will. But it's only a bad memory now. You hear what I'm saying, Ariel? It's over."

We can't forget, but we can live with it. That's what he was really saying, and he saw her slow nod of understanding.

Ariel looked once at Mast's body, then lifted her gaze to the ridge. "There's a place up there . . . a place he was holding me. Maybe I can find something dry to put on. And there's our horse he stole. . . ."

Parry said, "I saw where he left it." He tried to form a smile. "We're a ways from home, kid. But we'll make it back all right."

The nightmare had ended. They were the survivors. That, when you finally came down to it, was all that mattered.

ABOUT THE AUTHOR

T. V. Olsen is a longtime favorite western author who has seen many novels into print, including two, ARROW IN THE SUN and THE STALKING MOON, which were made into popular western movies. He has twice been nominated for Spur Awards by the Western Writers of America. Olsen lives with his wife, who is also a writer, in Wisconsin.

Tales of the West by T.V. OLSEN